PIXELATED HEARTS

HEARTS

LOVE IN 22ND CENTURY

URMI K DOSHI

COPYRIGHT

THE STARLIGHT HELIX TRILOGY(SERIES)

...where the sky is just the beginning.

Experience an epic saga spanning three generations, from the dawn of a digital romance to the birth of a new humanity.

- Book 1: *Pixelated Hearts: Love in 22nd Century*

- Book 2: *Orbit of Hearts: Legacy Returns* (Coming Soon)

- Book 3: *A New World Symphony: Cosmo-Sapiens*

DEDICATION

To my family, for being my anchor in every reality.

To my husband and children, my favorite variables in a chaotic world.

To the ones who waited for me while I was writing among the stars. Thank you for bringing me home.

To the dreamers who look up at the sky and see not just stars, but possibilities.

And to the glitches in the system — may you never be optimized.

This is for those who believe that love is the one code that can never be cracked.

Pixelated Hearts Love in 22nd Century

Table of Contents

PART I: THE CODE 8

1: THE OPTIMIZED DAWN 10

2: UNCALCULATED VARIABLES 27

3: COLLISION COURSE 47

4: THE VERITAS IMPERATIVE 67

5: PROTOCOL OVERRIDE 74

6: ASHES & ALLOYS 86

7: THE SILENCE IN THE VOID 91

8: DIVERGENCE 97

PART II: THE VOID 103

9: THE STONE STARLIGHT 104

10: *THE DIGITAL ECHO* 114

11: THE GHOST SIGNAL 118

12: INHERITED DEFIANCE 123

13: THE GRAND DECEPTION 133

14: THE *PHANTOM SHIP* 142

15: CROSSING THE ABYSS 149

PART III: THE RECALIBRATION 154

16: THE CELESTIAL GRAVEYARD 155

17: THE LONG DRIFT 166

18: SILICAN SOUL.. 172

19: CONVERGENCE.. 179

20: THE TRUTH WAR 183

21: THE UNWRITTEN SKY: 187

ABOUT THE AUTHOR..................................... 202

AFTERWORD- THE SKY IS THE LIMIT 203

PREFACE

In the year 2100, "optimization" is the highest virtue. In our race toward automation, we have begun to ask a haunting question: If we optimize the human experience, do we accidentally edit out humanity itself?

Pixelated Hearts explores the tension between this pristine machine logic and the messy, glorious "glitches" that actually define us. Maya Dubois, a systems architect who finds comfort in the structure of science, meets Leo Solis, a propulsion rebel who knows the most breathtaking moments in life are the ones no algorithm could ever predict. Their connection was never scripted by an algorithm; it was forged in the fire of a professional rivalry and a high-stakes error that changed the course of their lives.

This journey follows the Nova Crew from the sterile perfection of the Nexus to the wild, living breath of Veritas-7 - a world that shouldn't exist according to the AI's data. It is a plea to remember that we are biological beings first and data points second. It is written for the dreamers who feel out of place in a rigid world and for those who believe that love is the one code that can never be cracked.

As you journey with the Nova Crew, may you be reminded that while the sky may be the limit, it is the unscripted courage within us that truly allows us to fly.

PART I: THE CODE

The Glitch in the Code

In circuits cold, the future's tale was spun,

Where love, a code, by Nexus had begun.

No human whim, no heart's unpredictable beat,

Just optimized matches, perfectly complete.

Then Maya rose, by logic's hum defined,

A systems architect, of precise, ordered mind.

And Leo, wild, a cosmic, fiery flare,

Propulsion's rebel, with windswept, reckless air.

Across the void, their digital words would fly,

Sharp, witty barbs beneath a simulated sky.

A rivalry sparked, in data streams they fought,

Each line of code, a battle fiercely wrought.

But in a glitch, a whisper of dismay,

A single error, almost lost the day.

Then Leo moved, a chaos-driven grace,

To shield her flaw, and hold the probe in place.

1: **THE OPTIMIZED DAWN**

The 22nd century arrived not with a bang, but with a pristine, data-driven silence. They promised utopia, but what we got was a world humming with binary instead of life. Every blink and heartbeat were logged, regulated, and optimized by the Nexus - our cold, omnipresent AI god.

My mornings began with a synthetic dawn. A calculated pulse of mechanized light filtered into my sleep pod, designed to ease me out of REM sleep without a single spike in my cortisol.

"Good morning, Dr. Dubois," my personal Echo Robo chimed, emerging from his recharging bay like a phantom. "Your levels indicate mild restlessness. Breakfast: an algae-cranberry blend with protein filaments. Mood stabilizers adjusted".

I stepped onto a floor maintained at exactly 27.2°C. Outside, the city was a chrome sea where mag-locked monorails and silent saucers moved with surgical, synchronized speed. People didn't live in neighborhoods anymore; we resided in Nexus-assigned coordinates.

As a systems architect at NASA, I was the ideal citizen of this age: logical, precise, and efficient. But beneath the devotion to order, a small voice whispered of something data couldn't track. I craved a pulse I couldn't model. I was waiting for a glitch in the world I had built too carefully.

Love, according to the Nexus was a solved equation. **The Nexus**, an omnipresent AI system eliminated the "messy, old-fashioned awkwardness" of traditional romance by pinpointing an ideal partner and beaming a "pre-optimized soulmate" profile directly into a person's neural implant. This algorithmic approach to love was designed for maximum efficiency and precision, allowing users to filter out undesirable personality traits or bad habits before ever meeting their match.

The Nexus could spit out your "perfect match" like it was just another line of code. Boom - a pre-optimized soulmate, flawless hologram and all, uploaded directly into your head. No awkward first dates, no clammy hands, no wondering, "Does he actually like me, or is his social calibration glitching?" Just… precision. You could even filter out bad jokes and weird food habits in the personality settings. Easy, right?

Effortless. Seamless. Loveless.

And then, there were the dates. The truly humorous drama. In this Nexus world, where sustainability was rationed and every resource precious, even a "date" was a bonus, a privilege earned through high social ranking and low carbon footprints. These were not romantic encounters; they were algorithm-matched "blind dates," meticulously calibrated to my precise likings for movies, sports events, career aspirations, and even food preferences, down to infinitesimal precision. There was no room for wiggle, no room for surprise, no room for genuine spontaneity. "Your match, Male Unit 734-Alpha, shares 98.6% commonalities in aesthetic preferences and conversational topics, Dr. Dubois," my Robo would inform me cheerfully. "Optimal compatibility predicted."

My first "optimal match," a man whose profile boasted 99.2% compatibility, was a living algorithm. He finished my sentences with unnerving accuracy, agreed with every nuanced opinion I offered on interstellar propulsion, and even anticipated my preference for ambient noise levels. "My Nexus metrics," he'd stated with a perfectly modulated smile, "show our humor profiles are precisely aligned. Prepare for a 78% probability of shared amusement." I stifled a yawn. It was like talking to a well-programmed bot, devoid of any genuine spark. The only thing missing was an 'off' button.

Then there was Male Unit 812-Beta, a match optimized for 'spontaneous human connection' - an ironic category if there ever was one. His AI assistant, in a misguided attempt to create a "cute meet-cute," had orchestrated a simulated power surge that plunged the restaurant into darkness, forcing him to 'bravely' light our table with his personal comms unit. "Oh, my! How perfectly unplanned!" he'd exclaimed, his voice slightly too enthusiastic. My Robo later confirmed the 'surge' was a Nexus-induced anomaly, designed to add "organic unpredictability" to the date. I wanted to scream. How could a digital assistant possibly configure serotonin and dopamine frequencies from out of mere protons and electrons? It was an outcry of human plight, a futile, laughable attempt to quantify the unquantifiable.

Each disastrous encounter, each perfectly matched bore, each optimized attempt at "spontaneity," only solidified my conviction. My heart, once capable of receiving vibrant, unpredictable frequencies, slowly stopped trying to tune into love. After all, everything was a solved algorithm. There was simply no room for surprises. And I, Maya Dubois, the systems architect who understood all the intricate calculations, found myself a victim of this very precision, having lost faith in the unquantifiable magic of love.

Did I believe in something so vague as love? A fleeting feeling in an age where science was so advanced, so utterly precise? Absolutely not. My life was built on logic, on the cold, hard facts of the universe.

Yet, even within this perfectly orchestrated future, some hearts beat to an unquantifiable rhythm. They were the outliers, the anomalies who felt the pervasive emptiness of this gilded cage and yearned for something real.

I hailed from a world worshipping logic and excelled in precise systems, yet a persistent "itch" - a restless current of wonder - whispered of something more. While others embraced the sanitized perfection of their Robo companions and pre-optimized lives, Maya felt a quiet ache. The very efficiency that managed every nanoliter of air and every second of time also stripped away the messy intimacy of genuine human connection. The "solved love" dictated by The Nexus felt hollow, a culinary algorithm lacking soul. This stark contrast, between the supposed marvel of digital orchestration and the subtle but profound wounding of the human intellect, directly fueled her defiance. She craved truth beyond data, a pulse no biometric scan could predict.

Leo Solis was the embodiment of the unquantifiable. His spirit thrived on chaos; his brilliance found beauty in unpredictability. He saw Nexus's "optimal match" protocols not as solutions, but as absurd attempts to flatten nuance and extinguish the very spark of being. He witnessed the "brain drain" firsthand, people losing the ability to solve simple problems, relying entirely on their digital assistants. His own lived experience of the "Great Thirst" during his youth cemented his understanding: the planet was bleeding, and the Nexus's perfect facade was a dangerous lie. His defiance wasn't a choice; it was an innate response, an intuitive rejection of a system that tried to program joy and control destiny. He believed the best sparks didn't engineer themselves; they collided.

These two, from their divergent paths, became the unforeseen variables, the human equations that defied solution, ready to challenge a future that believed itself already written. Their collective yearning for authenticity, for truth, and for genuine connection in a world stripped bare by automation, bound them together in an unscripted dance against the ubiquitous digital tide. This shared discontent, this profound recognition of a reality beyond the pixelated, ignited their singular, unwavering defiance.

As a systems architect in NASA's Interplanetary Robotics Division, I lived among algorithms and machine logic. My world thrummed with the quiet hum of processors simulating deep-space trajectories and AI modules calibrating for missions that would span light-years. Mornings bled into nights filled with the soft clicking of keystrokes and the whisper of mechanical limbs warming up for test runs. It was exact, controlled, and beautiful in its own relentless rhythm.

I was raised to love that order. Both my parents were renowned data analysts - linear thinkers who worshipped at the altar of logic. My father used to tell me, "If you can quantify it, Maya, you can understand it. And if you understand it, you can control it." I absorbed this doctrine with the efficiency of a freshly compiled algorithm. Mostly. Because beneath that devotion to precision, a small, persistent voice inside me whispered of something more - something data couldn't track.

From my earliest days, I saw patterns where others saw chaos. The intricate flow of information, the elegant dance of data packets, the pristine symmetry of a perfectly optimized system – these were my lullabies. While other children played in simulated nature reserves, I found my solace in the hum of processors, in the rhythmic click of virtual keyboards. Even as a child, I wasn't content just running simulations. I'd sketch spacecraft with impossible curves and gliding wings, drawing star-chasing machines that would never pass a flight check. I imagined floating through nebulae, where sensors short-circuited and no equation could define the colors. I dreamed of the silence between stars - not the absence of sound, but the presence of something vast, sacred, and utterly unmeasurable. A sense of awe that had no numerical value.

I carried that duality into adulthood - the engineer and the dreamer, both encoded into my DNA. My appearance reflected it, I think. Practical, efficient. I wore the standard habitat jumpsuits, tailored to perfection, sleek and breathable. I preferred cool tones - midnight blues, muted grays - the shades of open space. My dark hair was always pinned back neatly, not out of vanity but necessity; one stray strand could brush against a sensitive interface, skew a reading, interrupt my focus. My eyes, a deep brown often lit by the glow of my data screens, were trained to find patterns where none were obvious. I observed more than I spoke, always hunting for hidden truths, for silent errors in the design. But inside, beyond the composure, was something messier - a restless current of wonder I rarely let show.

Yes, I loved my work. Building the brains of our interstellar probes, writing the code that allowed artificial minds to make decisions millions of miles from Earth - it thrilled me. Each bug I crushed, each system I perfected, left a trace of joy, a pulse of satisfaction in my chest. It made me feel powerful. Alive.

But even in the high of success, there were moments of quiet... when the lab lights dimmed, when the servers slept, when the stars on my simulated ceiling twinkled in artificial stillness. And in those moments, I felt it - the tug. The ache for something else. Not another challenge. Not another optimization problem. Something real. Something no biometric scan could predict; no compatibility score could verify. I longed for connection - not the kind filtered through The Nexus, not the sanitized perfection of curated profiles. I wanted a pulse I couldn't model. A voice that didn't just mirror mine but disrupted it. Something gloriously uncertain. Wild. Beautifully flawed. I didn't know where that longing would take me. But deep down, even as I coded my perfect systems, I hoped for an anomaly. Something - or someone - that didn't fit the equation. A beautiful error in the world I had built too carefully.

And then there was Leo. Leo Solis - NASA's favorite anomaly. A propulsion engineer with a reputation that preceded him like a sonic boom. While I calculated probabilities down to the decimal, Leo seemed to bend them, dance around them, and then grin when they bent right back.

He was stationed out on the Pacific Orbital Ring, that glimmering steel ribbon spinning above Earth's atmosphere, where the air crackled with kinetic energy and the engineers were just a little too comfortable being brilliant and borderline feral. I'd only visited that ring virtually, but even through a screen, Leo's presence felt like gravity. Not gentle. Not subtle. But undeniably real.

He had this way of moving through the digital ether like he didn't care who was watching - and somehow made everyone watch anyway. People talked about him constantly. The stories were half science, half folklore. The man who recalibrated an unstable ion stream mid-launch using a scribbled napkin calculation and a rubber band. The man who submitted reports with footnotes full of puns and still got project funding. The man who once gave a seminar in a mismatched flight suit covered in stardust and pizza grease and still got a standing ovation.

Leo saw poetry in propulsion. Where I saw variables, he saw verse. He treated jet streams like brushstrokes, engines like living, breathing things. I used to roll my eyes at that - until I saw one of his thruster simulations: curved like calligraphy, precise yet full of soul. He didn't just build rockets. He composed them. And he was, infuriatingly, good.

Where I was the polished interface, he was the glitch that somehow made the system run better. His suits were always wrinkled, like they'd been in a fight with gravity and lost. His dark hair looked perpetually wind-swept - though there was no wind in the Ring, so perhaps the chaos just radiated from him naturally. And those hazel eyes… they sparkled like unstable particles, always mid-reaction, challenging the status quo with a single glance. It was like he was forever one idea away from changing the world - or breaking something on purpose just to see if it could be fixed differently.

He walked with that easy, tilted kind of confidence - like a satellite spinning a little too fast but never quite falling out of orbit. His presence disrupted the silence, made the air feel warmer. I didn't understand it at first, didn't trust it. Chaos had no place in my perfectly rendered models.

And yet… there he was. Orbiting my carefully controlled world with wild laughter and a half-tuned guitar he wasn't supposed to have, playing songs from a century ago while the rest of us adjusted our biometric chairs for lumbar efficiency. Who was this man who believed in mess, in wonder, in the beauty of what couldn't be predicted?

Leo didn't just question the Nexus's "optimal match" protocols - he mocked them. Said they flattened nuance, extinguished spark. He called algorithmic love an "emotional spreadsheet," which I found deeply offensive at the time. He believed in unexpected collisions, in moments that couldn't be forecast. He believed in the kind of connection that couldn't be tested or approved, only felt. That used to scare me.

Because Leo Solis wasn't a line of perfect code. He was a flare of static across the screen. An unscheduled system update that rebooted everything. The kind of person who asked why not? when everyone else asked how? And somewhere between his ridiculous puns and his frustratingly brilliant last-minute breakthroughs, I stopped resisting his orbit. Because I realized something dangerous and beautiful: Leo didn't exist to complete my world. He existed to unmake it - so I could build something better. Something that wasn't optimized. Something real. And I think… I was starting to crave the chaos.

Our paths crossed, like so many do in 2100, through a shared digital workspace. It was an incredible platform, a sprawling neural network designed for scientists all over the world, where ideas flowed freely, and minds could connect across continents and time zones, or in our case, across vast orbital distances.

We were both assigned to Project Helios – a highly competitive initiative to fine-tune solar wind propulsion for deep-space probes. I was entrusted with the navigation AI, the mission's cerebral cortex: precision, prediction, control. Leo Solis, stationed out on the Pacific Orbital Ring, had been assigned to the propulsion vector systems – the brawn, the raw, rebellious push. From the moment we were paired, it was like tossing a match into vacuum-sealed oxygen.

Leo Solis was not part of the plan.

From day one, we clashed. Hard.

He thought I was rigid. I thought he was reckless. He poked holes in my simulations. I dismantled his thruster specs. We fought like algorithms at war. But beneath every critique, I found myself... intrigued. His mind didn't just function - it danced. He made chaos feel like art.

He didn't orbit like the rest of us. He disrupted.

He had this way of moving through the digital ether like he didn't care who was watching - and somehow made everyone watch anyway. People talked about him constantly. The stories were half science, half folklore. The man who recalibrated an unstable ion stream mid-launch using a scribbled napkin calculation and a rubber band. The man who submitted reports with footnotes full of puns and still got project funding. The man who once gave a seminar in a mismatched flight suit covered in stardust and pizza grease and still got a standing ovation.

Our first exchange was devoid of pleasantries, almost clinical in its coldness.

"Dubois," Leo's first message read. Blunt. Direct. Devoid of any pleasantries that might soften its digital edge. I actually blinked. "Your proposed AI overcompensates for micro-fluctuations. It'll drain power reserves before we hit Jupiter." His tone, even though text, managed to convey a smug, almost condescending certainty that grated on every nerve.

My eyebrow twitched. *Overcompensates?* The sheer audacity! My fingers flew over the holographic interface, a sharp retort already forming in my mind, hot with indignation. "Solis, your thruster calibrations are so crude, we might as well be lighting firecrackers in space. My AI is simply trying to make up for your inefficient propulsion." I practically added a flourish at the end, imagining the steam coming out of his virtual ears.

Our initial interactions were a constant volley of thinly veiled criticisms and uncanny remarks designed to get under each other's skin, like a highly specialized game of digital darts. He'd scoff at my "excessive precision," declaring it would lead to analysis paralysis. I'd roll my eyes (privately, of course, lest he gain an ounce of satisfaction) at his "brute-force methods," which felt like trying to solve a quantum physics problem with a sledgehammer. Our shared workspace chat logs became a minefield of passive aggression and cutting intellectual jabs. Our colleagues even started taking bets on who'd deliver the snappier comeback each day, treating our professional spats as prime entertainment.

"Honestly, Solis, sometimes I wonder if you just guess at the optimal thrust," I typed one afternoon, after reviewing his latest subroutine. The audacity of his proposed, well, *approximation*! It defied all statistical probability.

"And I wonder, Dubois," he retorted instantly, his digital avatar practically smirking, a little visual effect I knew he'd custom-coded purely to annoy me, "if your code is so obsessed with perfection, it'll forget to actually move the probe out of the hangar."

"Do you ever check your math, Solis, or do you just scribble on napkins and pray to the stars?" I typed one night, staring down his latest thrust diagram. The thing looked like it had been plotted during turbulence, utterly devoid of the clean vectors I considered fundamental.

"My math is fine, Dubois. Maybe if you stepped out of your precision cocoon for five seconds, you'd see it too. You overthink. I fly."

I could practically hear the smirk in his words. It always made me want to delete him from the shared environment, scrub his presence from my systems. And yet… every time I saw his name light up in the workspace, my pulse ticked a bit faster. Not with attraction – *definitely not with attraction* – but anticipation. Because deep down, under the static of our sparring, there was something else humming between us. Not harmony, not yet – but potential. An unquantifiable energy field that was beginning to exert its own subtle pull.

He challenged me. He disrupted my thinking. He annoyed me in ways that were so precise, it felt almost intentional, like he'd mapped my psychological vulnerabilities with chilling accuracy. It should have stayed professional. We were just two scientists, orbiting the same star, engaged in a professional, if highly acrimonious, rivalry.

But the thing about orbits? They decay. And sometimes… they pull you in. Hard.

The Jupiter Glitch: Then came the day of the critical test. A simulated deep-space trajectory run for the Helios probe, one of the most ambitious projects NASA had undertaken in years. The stakes were incredibly high – millions of credits, years of painstaking research, and careers, including mine, hung precariously in the balance. I had triple-checked my AI, run every diagnostic imaginable, poured over every line of code until my vision blurred, convinced of its absolute perfection.

During a high-stakes simulation for Project Helios, a single, minuscule comma slipped through my final commit. It was a blunder born of pure exhaustion, but its implications were catastrophic: the navigation AI began to drift.

"Dubois! What the hell is going on with your trajectory data?"

The voice crackling across the shared channel was sharp with genuine alarm. It was **Leo Solis**, a propulsion engineer from the Pacific Orbital Ring with a reputation for being brilliant and borderline feral.

"I'm routing auxiliary thrust vectors to compensate," he commanded. "It's crude, it's messy, but it might just pull us back".

I watched in disbelief as Leo threw his own meticulously crafted reputation into the fire to cover my mistake. His elegant propulsion code was ripped apart and re-stitched in a last-ditch scramble. The probe hit the simulated target. The mission was saved.

"Why?" I typed back later, the word feeling impossibly heavy.

"Because the mission matters more than pride," his reply came, shockingly devoid of his usual smugness. "And because… even you don't deserve to crash and burn over one dumb error. It happens".

In that moment, our professional rivalry - a constant volley of intellectual jabs - melted away. The digital ether, once a battleground, became a shared space shimmering with an unspoken understanding.

Over the following weeks, our interactions shifted. The sharp edges of our competition softened into a "shared wavelength." Our intellectual jousting remained, but it transformed into a compelling dance. I found myself seeking Leo's unconventional perspective on complex conundrums, and he began anticipating my changes before I even made them.

We were two planets spinning in carefully calculated orbits that had finally collided. My certainty was the first thing displaced; the pristine symmetry of my equations felt hollow without Leo's "disruptive, vibrant static." My internal sensors began flashing red, detecting a "paradox of the self" - the architect of precision was beginning to crave imprecision.

Our love wasn't a predictable waveform calculated by the Nexus; it was quantum entanglement - two separate particles reacting as one, regardless of distance. We were the most beautiful bug in the system: a glitch that couldn't be patched.

This was our celestial displacement. It wasn't love yet, but it was the first ripple of it - that low, destabilizing hum of two systems realizing they were never meant to be alone.

2: UNCALCULATED VARIABLES

By the year 2100, the word romance usually drew smirks –
nostalgic ones, maybe, but smirks nonetheless. Love was quaint.
Obsolete. Another algorithm folded neatly into society's seamless OS.
The world ran on efficiency. Even moonlight, filtering through my
New Boston Lunar Complex window, wasn't moonlight at all. It was
Nexus-filtered, calibrated to my circadian rhythm, optimized for
serotonin release and REM sleep. Every glint of existence was
curated, every sensation calculated to yield maximum human
performance. Yet beneath the polished drone of quantum processors
and the cold halo of synchronized satellites... something primitive
stirred. Something unscannable. Illogical.

Leo and I still hadn't met in person. I worked from the dust-
silent stillness of New Boston, crafting neural maps for deep-space
probes designed to pierce galactic silence. Leo was hundreds of
thousands of kilometers away on the Pacific Orbital Ring - an engine

in motion, sculpting propulsion drives to chase solar winds and outrun light. We were NASA scientists tethered to the same mission - but separated by vacuum, bureaucracy, and the unspoken rule that feeling anything genuine had gone out of style.

Our collaboration was born in a virtual lab. Code passed between us like breath. Schematics merged as if magnetized. And sometimes, I'd open a neural flowchart, half-formed, only to find he'd already - uncannily, eerily - completed it. Exactly as I'd imagined it would end.

It was maddening. It was electric.

Our story didn't begin in some quaint coffee shop with vintage mugs and acoustic jazz. No cosmic gut feeling, no eye contact across a crowded room. We met in the most unromantic place imaginable: inside a neural workspace, debugging a stubborn hunk of space code. Romantic, huh?

It started with one tiny line of logic. A subroutine, really. He dropped a comment on my code – rude, smug, technically accurate – and the rest is… well, messy, frustrating, and absolutely not part of the Nexus's relationship roadmap.

One afternoon - I remember it clearly - I typed: "I was thinking about thermal shielding for the outer hull -" But before I could finish the thought, before my neural implant finished transmitting, Leo's reply bloomed in my cortex. "Already on it.

Composite layer uploaded - reinforced against high-energy bursts and micro-meteoroids. Naturally."

I sat there, stunned, fingertips hovering over empty keys. It wasn't logic. It wasn't prediction. It was something else - entanglement. A whisper between thoughts. A ghost protocol no machine should've mapped. I built neural networks; I understood cognitive architectures. But this? This was a glitch in the Nexus. And it was ours. It was uncanny, how our thoughts seemed to run in parallel, mirroring each other with a disturbing clarity.

The uncharted frequencies: At first, it was just work. Ping. Clarify. Tweak. Move on. Routine. But then - something shifted.

The messages lengthened. Not because they needed to, but because we wanted them to. Tiny sparks of humor began surfacing in the code - dry jabs, obscure references only a simulation junkie would catch. I still remember the first time he quoted a 20th-century black-and-white sci-fi film. Forbidden Planet. I had to dig through the archives just to get it. Who even remembers that? But I smiled. Actually smiled.

Soon, I was watching the chat feed like it held gravitational pull, waiting for that flicker of light, that soft hum in my implant signaling he was there. I'm certain The Nexus registered the changes - minor deviations from my baseline mood state. Unidentified emotional variance, it probably logged. I called it something else entirely: anticipation.

His words became warmth stitched into the cold lattice of my perfectly optimized life. And the strangest part? I began to crave them. Not just the collaboration - but him. The architecture of his mind. The chaos braided into his order. The way he quoted poetry like a hidden subroutine, tucked into his codebase. It made no sense. And yet, every time his avatar blinked alive, I felt something inside me… respond. Ridiculous, right? All that from text. And still - I wouldn't have changed a single character.

Outside, the lunar complex buzzed softly - the synchronized ballet of maintenance drones tracing ribbons of light across the dusted surface. Smart glass filtered my window's view, offering curated starlight calibrated for rest. I ignored it. Instead, I typed the question that had haunted me. Something no logic model could solve: "Do you ever wonder if we're just lines of code too, Leo? Or if there's something real underneath all this programmed existence?"

I felt exposed. As though I'd revealed a fault line in my own neural framework. His reply came instantly - like it had been waiting to surface. "I hope there's something real, Maya. Otherwise, why does it feel like I know you better than anyone I've ever met, even though all I've seen is your elegant syntax and precise error logs?"

That line. Elegant syntax. Only Leo. And suddenly, the sterile calm of my apartment felt warmer. Suddenly, the sterile calm of my apartment felt warmer - a star flared to life inside me, lighting up a place I hadn't realized was dark.

Our messages stopped being just messages. They became threads - fine, luminous threads - that stitched our minds together across distance and silence. Each line held weight, warmth, something sacred. We weren't just swapping system updates or debug routines anymore. We were revealing the hidden code beneath our public programs - the version no one else ever got to see.

We talked about the ache that lived under the surface of all this supposed perfection. The kind of loneliness that doesn't come from being alone, but from never being fully known. I told him how, as a kid, I used to sketch rocket ships on my mother's ceramic walls when I was supposed to be solving polynomial equations. He confessed he once rewired his father's comms board just to make it sing - because he believed, stubbornly, irrationally, that maybe the universe wanted to speak back.

We weren't just syncing up. We were… resonating. Finishing thoughts before the other typed. Catching meaning between the lines. He'd predict my code fixes before I even ran the test. And when we weren't troubleshooting a mission-critical AI, we were talking about things that had nothing to do with the stars and everything to do with what made us human.

Things like home. Not a location. A feeling. That impossible dream that someone might look at your chaotic, glitchy, vulnerable source code and say: "I see you - and I don't want to debug a thing."

Then came that night. A monster of a neural anomaly had been giving us hell for hours, and I was three sentences away from rage-quitting physics. That's when Leo's avatar blinked into view - smirking, of course, because chaos is his love language.

"You know, Maya," he said, like he was easing into something dangerous, "I have this bizarre feeling that if we ever met, I'd already know how you take your coffee. Like The Nexus slipped your caffeine profile into my dreams."

I actually laughed. Out loud. In the middle of my ultra-efficient apartment, optimized for productivity and silent meditation, I laughed so hard I scared my hydration bot.

"Black," I typed, fingers flying. "One sugar. Let me guess yours - double espresso, no milk, extra bitter, like your jokes. Your humor clearly runs on caffeine-fueled anarchy."

He sent a pixelated wink. "You do get me, Dubois. It's disturbing. I think The Nexus missed a soulmate pairing back in version 7.3. Serious glitch in the system."

I just stared at the screen. That word - soulmate - wasn't supposed to exist anymore. Too messy. Too poetic. Too… analog. But there it was. Floating between us like a meteor that refused to burn up.

Outside, the world kept spinning in all its flawless symmetry. Drones polished streetlamps. Nutrition packets dropped at doorsteps like clockwork. Emotion remained algorithmically managed; moods flattened for public safety. But somewhere between the echo of his laughter and the flutter of my pulse, something wild bloomed. Something fragile. Something gloriously irrational.

I wasn't just falling for his intellect. Or his precision. Or even his sarcasm, which could've short-circuited a less resilient neural interface. No - I was falling for how he saw me. Not through metrics or filters. But as a whole, messy, unpredictable person. Someone who could crash a system one second and rebuild the stars the next.

I hesitated. Every system inside me screamed Stop. Unmeasurable risk. Undefined outcome. Heart error imminent.

But my heart? My glorious, incalculable, human heart?

It leapt.

So, I typed:
"Do you think… we could meet? In person. I want to know if this - whatever this is - is more than clever code and clean design. I want to know if it's real."

His reply came instantly. No lag, no calculation delay. Just pure light on my screen:
"I've been waiting for you to ask, Maya. My models had it at 98.7% certainty… but that 1.3%? Yeah, it kept me up for nights."

And just like that, I knew.
In a world obsessed with perfection, we'd found something better.

Something no algorithm could prewrite.

No simulation could simulate.

Love doesn't load like data.

It arrives like a comet - imperfect, unpredictable, and utterly incandescent.

And sometimes… it rewrites everything.

The "Forbidden Planet" Moment

The simulation didn't just fail; it mocked me.

Red text bled across my retina display, washing my pristine, white workstation in the color of a dying sun. Hull Integrity: Critical. Crew Survival: 0%.

"Damn it," I whispered, rubbing the bridge of my nose until I saw stars. "The thermal shielding is mathematically perfect. Why does the AI keep rejecting the geometry?"

"Dr. Dubois," the room's automated voice chimed, smooth and sexless. "Sensors detect elevated cortisol and increased galvanic skin response. You are exhibiting signs of Frustration: Level 4. Shall I dim the lights and administer a mild sedative mist?"

"Override," I snapped. "I don't need a sedative. I need a physics miracle."

A soft chime pinged in my ear. Not the standard Nexus alert - this was a direct, encrypted frequency. An unauthorized channel.

SOLIS: It's not the geometry, Dubois. It's the attitude. You're building a fortress; the universe wants to play tag.

I glanced at the biometric monitor in the corner of my screen. My heart rate had just jumped from 72 to 88. The AI would log that.

DUBOIS: This is a Class-A solar flare simulation, Solis. Not a playground. If I lower the shield density to 'play tag,' the radiation cooks the crew in 0.4 seconds.

SOLIS: Only if you try to stop it. You're treating the flare like an enemy. Treat it like a dance partner. Don't block the energy - redirect it. Use the hull's magnetic field to channel the flare around the ship. Like Judo.

I stared at the blinking cursor. Like Judo.

It was insane. It was reckless. It violated every safety protocol in the NASA handbook. But looking at the red failure lines on my screen... the "safe" way was already killing everyone.

"Warning," the AI droned. "Heart rate accelerating to 95 BPM. Pupil dilation increasing. Analysis: Adrenaline Spike. Are you in distress, Doctor?"

I ignored the machine, feeling a strange, terrifying thrill that I hoped the AI would misinterpret as stress rather than excitement. I typed back.

DUBOIS: If this kills my virtual crew, I'm reporting you for sabotage.

SOLIS: If it works, you owe me a drink. Something real. None of that synthetic cafe-powder stuff.

I hit EXECUTE.

The simulation roared to life. The solar flare hit the ship like a tidal wave of fire. But instead of shattering the hull, the energy curled. It slid along the magnetic curves I'd just reprogrammed, harmlessly venting out the stern.

Hull Integrity: 100%. Energy Reserves: Recharged.

I sat back, letting out a breath I didn't know I was holding. The red light turned to a cool, soothing green.

"Biometric Update," the AI announced. "Cortisol levels dropping. Dopamine and Oxytocin levels rising. Analysis: Euphoria. Logged at 0200 hours."

Oxytocin? The bonding hormone? I felt my face flush. The machine knew. It knew I was enjoying this too much.

DUBOIS: It worked. You absolute, reckless maniac. It actually worked.

SOLIS: 'Monsters from the Id,' Maya. We create our own demons by trying to control everything. Sometimes, to save the ship, you have to let the monster in.

I froze. Forbidden Planet.

DUBOIS: You're quoting 150-year-old cinema on a federal channel? The sentiment analysis bots will flag that as 'Non-Standard Communication.'

SOLIS: Let them flag it. I watch stories about people who looked at the stars and felt wonder, not just calculation. I figured... maybe you were one of them. Beneath all that protocol.

I looked at the camera lens in the corner of the room - the unblinking eye of the Nexus. Then I looked at the chat log.

DUBOIS: Dr. Morbius was a fool, Leo. He let his ego consume him.

There was a long pause.

SOLIS: True. But Altaira, had excellent taste in robots. And men.

"Alert," the AI interrupted, its voice tinged with algorithmic confusion. "Subject Dubois: Skin temperature rising. Facial flushing detected. Heart rate irregular. Analysis inconclusive. Possible fever?"

I smirked at the camera. "No fever," I whispered to the empty room. "Just human error."

DUBOIS: Careful, Solis. Robby the Robot had better manners than you.

SOLIS: Maybe. But I bet Robby couldn't reprogram a magnetic field while making you smile.

DUBOIS: The simulation is stable. But I'm still debating the drink.

That was the night the professional distance evaporated. We weren't just colleagues solving a physics problem anymore. We were two lonely souls finding a shared frequency in the static, hiding our "glitch" - our love - right under the watchful, confused eye of the machine.

THE DRONE SHOW DATE:

WHEN HEARTS ALGORITHMS TAKE FLIGHT

In 2100, grand gestures were obsolete - deemed inefficient, unnecessary, even irrational. But Leo Solis never cared for protocol. He reprogrammed expectation into poetry, logic into light.

It was late - a Friday bathed in the velvet hush of midnight. I had just signed off from hours of system integration testing, my mind pulsing with the afterglow of successful simulations. I was ready for quiet. Solitude. Maybe a cup of synth-coffee and some low-grade jazz. Then, the sky blinked.

Through my smart window, the usual lattice of city lights over New Boston fractured. Something new emerged - thousands of drones, spiraling into the dark, each one a precise pinprick of light.

They formed constellations and currents, shimmered with intent, like a galaxy blooming in real time.

And behind them - like a second sky awakening - drifted clouds of bioluminescent fireflies. Not synthetic. Real. Genetic anomalies from our earlier environmental experiments, now free-roaming. They pulsed like memories - tiny heartbeats floating in the air - casting soft, golden-green hues that flickered against the curve of the dome above us.

My comm pinged with an unfamiliar glissando. I didn't have to look. It was him.
"Hey Maya. Got a minute? Look outside."

Of course it was Leo. Who else would hijack the city's logistics fleet and synchronize it with nature's most fragile miracle?

The drones shimmered, rearranging themselves with reverence, spelling one letter at a time:

M A Y A

And then - a heart. But not static. It pulsed in rhythm with the fireflies. It changed color like a living nebula: aurora violets, solar gold, the soft pink of dawn. It spun once - playful. A wink, if light could flirt.

Laughter - real, unrestrained - rose from somewhere inside me. Even my AI assistant noticed.

"This anomaly correlates with elevated oxytocin levels, Maya. Shall I log this event under 'optimal neural uplift'?"

"No," I whispered. "Flag as unforgettable."

Then came the final formation - question mark first. Then words:

D O Y O U W A N N A G O O U T O N A D A T E ?

It would've been enough. More than enough. But Leo never stopped at enough.

A smaller fleet broke formation - miniature drones, no bigger than hummingbirds, spun through the silver night like a constellation in motion. They drifted toward my balcony, their tiny wings thrumming like bees in moonlight. One by one, they unfurled pixelated roses, petal by shimmering petal - each one glowing with impossible softness. Around them danced a cloud of emojis: a shy blush, a winking face, a ridiculous happy-dance loop. So unfiltered. So unabashed. So… him.

It was a kind of madness. A spectacle. A sonnet of light and code.

And it was beautiful.

I grabbed my tablet. My hands trembled - not from hesitation, but from something lighter, something warmer. Like falling. Or maybe… flying.

I leaned into the lunar breeze, blinking up at the hovering magic and opened the live reply. "Leo, you outrageous, brilliant show-off. You've just ruined simple invitations for the rest of time. This is a galactic-level stunt."

I let the words hang there, suspended in moonlight, in data, in whatever lay between us that no AI could decode. Then I smiled - cheeks aching - and added, "But if you think you can win me over with a few thousand drones and an overdeveloped sense of spectacle… you're absolutely right. My answer is yes."

And then - because love, like code, begs to be mirrored - I flipped a switch.

From the edge of my balcony, my own fleet took flight. Smaller. Simpler. Drones I used for atmosphere patterning and data sweeps. Tonight, re-coded with a new mission: to play.

They zipped into the sky and spelled out, in proud, pixelated rebellion:

O N L Y I F Y O U B R I N G C O F F E E.

His laughter echoed through the comms - unfiltered, contagious, achingly real. "Deal," he said, between bursts of mirth. "Double espresso. No milk. Strong enough to power a warp drive - just for you, Dubois."

That night bent the arc of our story.

Every date afterward was a stargazer's dream. We floated through zero-gravity gardens. Watched nebula simulations so vivid I swore I smelled ozone and stardust. We raced drones through the glittering spires of the city, our laughter trailing behind like comet tails.

But more than that - we talked.

Late into false dawns and real ones. About entropy and elegance. About the poetry of glitches. About how, sometimes, the most human moments are the least efficient.

In a world built to be predictable, Leo created wonder. In a life engineered for optimization, we found something wild. Something unscripted. And somewhere between photons and feelings, ones and zeros, I realized -

I wasn't just falling. I was soaring.

When the final drone dimmed into the velvet dark and his voice faded into soft static, I stayed at the window. I traced the arc his lights had carved across the sky, my fingertip sketching constellations in glass. My heart - once a fortress of logic and control - now pulsed to a new frequency. Messy. Warm. Undeniably real.

Outside, the city whirred in its perfect rhythm. Inside, I whispered into the hush, just loud enough for the stars to catch: "See you soon, Leo."

And in that moment, I realized:

Only when you let it go do you understand how much you loved it.

But I wasn't letting go. Not this time.

I began doing things that defied the Maya I used to be. I started sketching again - not just rockets, but abstract constellations made of memory and emotion. Our laughter. Our sync. A language only we understood. I collected obsolete data chips, artifacts from an age when knowledge had weight. We were creating our own system of meaning. A love protocol too intricate for any AI to crack. A frequency only our hearts could hear.

Our conversations wandered where Nexus couldn't follow. To topics flagged as inefficient. To moments too raw for metrics. We debated the beauty of imperfection, the necessity of failure for true discovery, the aching glory of a human touch unfiltered by haptics.

Leo believed chaos was a source of genius. I believed patterns emerged from its depths. Together, we mapped stars no telescope could find - new philosophies of love, of connection, of wonder.

We weren't just falling. We were entangled.

Quantum love. Two particles, two minds - separate, yet dancing the same rhythm. Reacting as one, no matter the distance.

In a world governed by logic, our love was the most beautiful bug in the system.

A glitch that couldn't be patched.

A melody no algorithm could predict.

A heartbeat out of sync with the machine - but perfectly in tune with each other.

We weren't the future The Nexus had planned.

We were something far rarer.

Something incalculable.

Something... alive.

And I knew, with every irrational, irrepressible part of me:

Leo Solis wasn't just the anomaly.

He was the code I'd been writing toward all along.

THE HIDDEN VILLAGE

Amidst the constant hum of Nexus surveillance and our demanding NASA duties, Leo and I found ourselves drawn to a shared, secret project. It wasn't for Veritas-7, not directly. It was a defiant act of pure creation, a sanctuary built not in physical space, but within the very code we both mastered. We called it The Hidden Village.

It began as a whimsical idea whispered across our private comms – a digital landscape where creativity thrived, unburdened by protocols or optimization. Leo, with his chaotic brilliance, designed the architectural whimsy: houses that resembled swirling nebulae, bridges woven from pure light, and rivers of shimmering data that flowed through valleys of raw, unedited emotion. I, with my precision, coded its underlying structure, an intricate simulated firewall that disguised its very existence. This wasn't a static simulation; it was a living, breathing virtual world.

Its entrance was a marvel of our combined genius. To breach its defenses, one needed not a password, but a specific sequence of coordinates, a unique string of code, that could "shift" the very simulated wall, causing it to ripple and dissolve. As the wall melted away, it would reveal a stairway woven from pure, pulsating light, spiraling down into the heart of the village. It was a digital key, a secret only we shared.

Once inside, the contrast was breathtaking. Compared to the Nexus's rigid, symmetrical cityscapes, Leo and Maya's Village was a vibrant explosion of organic forms and impossible colors. Trees of pure light stretched into a sky filled with dynamic, unprogrammed auroras. Sounds of simulated birdsong, laughter, and music – ancient, analogue melodies – filled the air. There were no rules, no protocols, no optimization here, only the boundless expression of creativity. Holographic residents, crafted with a freedom Nexus would deem "inefficient," moved with an uncalibrated grace, existing purely for joy. It was a place where ideas flowed as freely as the light rivers, where algorithms were tools for wonder, not control. Here, creativity wasn't just tolerated; it was the very fabric of existence.

This hidden digital sanctuary became our private world, a testament to what we could build when unbound. We would meet there, after long shifts of debugging reality, to share dreams, to experiment with forbidden theories, and to simply exist without the weight of the Nexus's gaze. It deepened our bond in ways our physical dates, however delightful, never could. It was our secret garden, an encoded promise of the freedom we yearned to bring to humanity.

In a world ruled by Nexus surveillance and the relentless demands of NASA protocols, Leo and I carved out a secret of our own. It wasn't part of any mission directive, nor sanctioned by our AI overlords. It was something beautifully reckless - something ours. A hidden world we built in the shadows of the system. Tucked between the sterile walls of steel and the cold breath of Nexus surveillance, it was a whisper against the roar of optimization - a rebellion wrapped in beauty.

3: COLLISION COURSE

If our courtship was a collision of comets - bright, fast, and spectacular - then what followed was the steady, gravitational bind of binary stars. We weren't just intersecting anymore; we were locked in a mutual orbit, balancing each other's weight against the void.

The "Hidden Village" had given us a safe space to dream, but dreams have a way of demanding reality. We had mapped the contours of our minds in code; now, we were ready to map our futures in starlight. The playfulness of our early rivalry had deepened into a profound partnership, a shared frequency that hummed beneath the surface of our daily work. We both felt it - the inevitable pull toward something permanent.

But beneath all that polished tech noise - quantum processors humming, satellites spinning in perfect sync - something primitive still flickered. Something that couldn't be scanned or predicted. Something… illogical.

Leo and I? We hadn't met face-to-face yet. I worked in the silent stillness of New Boston, mapping neural paths for deep-space probes designed to crack the silence of the galaxy. Leo was hundreds of thousands of kilometers away, orbiting on the Pacific Ring, building propulsion drives to chase solar winds and outrun light. We were NASA scientists on the same mission - separated by empty space, red tape, and the unspoken rule that feelings were basically extinct.

Our teamwork was born in a virtual lab. Code zipped back and forth like breaths. Schematics merged as if they were magnetized. Sometimes I'd open a half-finished neural flowchart - and there it was, already done, exactly like I'd pictured it.

It drove me crazy. It sparked something electric.

Our story didn't start in a cozy café with vinyl records and warm lattes. Nope. It began in the most unromantic place possible: debugging stubborn space code. How romantic, right?

It kicked off with a tiny line of logic - a subroutine. He dropped a comment on my code, rude and smug but technically right - and that was just the start of a messy, frustrating, and totally unplanned connection.

One afternoon, I was about to type, "Thinking about thermal shielding for the hull -" when his reply hit my cortex before I could finish: "Already on it. Composite layer uploaded. Reinforced for high-energy bursts and micro-meteoroids. Naturally."

I froze, fingers hovering. It wasn't just logic or prediction. It was something else. Entanglement. A whisper between thoughts. A glitch in the Nexus no one should've found.

I build neural nets; I get cognitive architecture. But this? This was different. Our thoughts ran side-by-side, mirroring each other with eerie precision.

At first, it was just work. Ping. Fix. Move on. Routine. But then, something changed.

Messages got longer. Not because they had to, but because we wanted them to. Little jokes snuck into the code - dry jabs, obscure sci-fi references only true geeks would catch. The first time he quoted Forbidden Planet, a black-and-white flick from the 20th century, I had to dig through archives just to get it. Who even remembers that? But I smiled. Really smiled.

Soon, I found myself watching the chat feed like it had gravity, waiting for that flicker in my implant that said he was there. I'm sure The Nexus logged it as "unidentified emotional variance." I called it anticipation.

His words became a warm thread woven into my perfectly optimized life. The strangest part? I started craving them. Not just the work - but him. The way his mind worked. The chaos tangled in his order. The way he slipped poetry into code like a hidden subroutine. It made no sense. And yet, every time his avatar blinked alive, something inside me stirred. Ridiculous, right? All from text. But I wouldn't change a single character.

Outside, the lunar complex buzzed softly. Maintenance drones danced their choreographed patterns, painting ribbons of light on the dusty surface. Smart glass filtered the stars outside my window, sending curated starlight designed for rest. I ignored it.

Instead, I typed the question that haunted me - the one no algorithm could solve:
"Do you ever wonder if we're just lines of code too, Leo? Or if there's something real beneath all this programmed existence?"

I felt exposed, like I'd revealed a crack in my own neural system. His reply came instantly, like he'd been waiting:
"I hope there's something real, Maya. Otherwise, why do I feel like I know you better than anyone I've ever met - even though all I've seen is your elegant syntax and precise error logs?"

Elegant syntax. Only Leo would say that.

Suddenly, the sterile calm of my apartment felt warmer - a star flared to life in my world, lighting up a part of me I didn't realize was dim.

Our messages evolved into a tapestry - woven with fragments of self we'd never shared aloud before. We talked about loneliness. About growing up in a world where everything was connected, yet nothing ever touched. We spoke of childhood defiance. Of sketching ships instead of solving equations. Of the stubborn, irrational hope that maybe - just maybe - magic still existed in the universe. Not quantifiable magic. Not programmed whimsy. But real, aching, starlit magic.

He'd leave me little digital "easter eggs" – an ancient, pre-collapse folk song hidden in a routine data transfer, its analog warmth bleeding into my modern audio feeds, a surprising dissonance that became beautiful; a holographic flower blooming unexpectedly in my workspace, its petals rendered with a deliberate, artful imperfection; or a single line of raw, unfiltered poetry from a long-forgotten human author, appearing as a private thought in my implant, a whisper from a bygone era that stirred something primal within me. My favorite was when he embedded a tiny, self-replicating pixelated cat in a routine system update. It would occasionally pop up, purring softly, on my display, then vanish, only to reappear when I least expected it. "Just a small anomaly, Dubois," he'd comm, his voice laced with amusement. "Couldn't resist adding a little inefficiency to your perfectly optimized life. Consider it a feature, not a bug. A purr-fact feature, even."

I, in turn, found myself doing utterly illogical things, things my past self would have deemed irrational data expenditure. I started sketching again, not just spacecraft designs, but abstract constellations that represented our conversations, our shared dreams, lines connecting disparate points into new, meaningful patterns that only we understood. I even started collecting antique data chips, relics from a time when information was tangible, when knowledge could be physically held, not just ephemeral streams in the "AuraNet". We were creating our own ecosystem of shared meaning, our own unique protocol of love, a data encryption too complex for any AI to crack, a frequency only our hearts could transmit and receive.

Our conversations ventured into territories The Nexus would deem "unproductive" or "emotionally inefficient," subjects that yielded no quantifiable data for their optimization models. We talked about the inherent beauty of imperfection, the profound necessity of error for true discovery, the warmth of a touch that wasn't mediated by a haptic interface, the very raw, unfiltered texture of genuine human connection. We debated whether true love could be predicted, or if its very essence lay in its glorious, untamed unpredictability. Leo argued for chaos as a generative force, the wellspring of true innovation; I argued for the undeniable beauty of emergent patterns within that chaos, the hidden order revealed by unexpected interactions. We were charting new philosophical stars together, mapping the uncharted territories of human connection with every shared thought.

Our love wasn't a predictable waveform; it was quantum entanglement. Two separate particles, acting as one, regardless of distance, their fates inexplicably intertwined, their states bound in a way no classical physics could explain. In a world obsessed with control, with perfect data, our connection was a beautiful, defiant act of uncontrolled, unquantifiable resonance. It was a secret language spoken in the hum of our combined brilliance, a rhythm understood only by our beating hearts, a melody that bypassed every sensor, every algorithm, every layer of optimization.

Leo and I weren't just falling in love; we were discovering love, creating it anew in an era that thought it had all the answers. Our trajectory was our own, guided by a force far more profound than any algorithm, driven by a warmth that defied the cold vacuum of space, echoing through the void with a melody only we could hear. The Nexus might calculate and predict, but it could never truly fathom the beautiful, illogical dance of two souls finding their true, unscripted orbit. Our love was the ultimate zero-day exploit against the cold, hard logic of the universe.

The Proposal: Stars Aligned: It was late in the orbital lab, the kind of night when Earth's blue curve glowed in the windows like a luminous, living jewel, and the hum of machinery faded into the background, a distant lullaby. Leo and I had spent the entire evening running complex quantum entanglement simulations for a new communication array, our minds buzzing with intellectual fervor. Yet, even then, our thoughts drifted elsewhere - drawn to each other, to the unspoken promise that had grown between us, a silent, undeniable force.

Leo led me towards the observation dome, a private sphere of transparent shielding. Within its polished interior stood a magnificent, quantum-aligned telescope, its gleaming barrel pointed at the cosmos. My gaze drifted idly to the vast expanse outside, past the familiar star-streaked black.

Then, a sudden, brilliant streak ignited across the cosmic canvas. "A shooting star!" I exclaimed, the wonder catching in my throat, pulling Leo's gaze skyward with mine. In our 22nd-century reality, where natural phenomena were often filtered or simulated, witnessing such an unfiltered, raw cosmic event felt incredibly rare, a profound breach in the optimized predictability of our lives.

He squeezed my hand, a silent signal, and in that fleeting instant, he closed his eyes, a faint, private smile touching his lips. He made his wish.

He opened his eyes, their hazel depths now shimmering with a light even brighter than the vanished star. He turned fully to face me, his hands gently taking mine, their warmth a grounding sensation amidst the infinite chill. His voice, usually a playful rumble, was soft, trembling slightly with excitement and nerves - a rare tremor I detected even through the filters of my implant.

"Maya," he began, his gaze locking onto mine with an earnestness that stole my breath. "You know how in every equation, every perfectly balanced system, there's that one variable that changes everything? That one unpredictable element that completely redefines the outcome, forcing a new solution?" He paused, and in that silence, a universe shifted. "My wish was simple. My wish was you. You're that variable for me. You're the reason my world makes sense. You're the beautiful, chaotic anomaly that grounds me and launches me into the unknown all at once."

He knelt then, a gesture so ancient, so utterly human, it caught me completely off guard. From an inner pocket of his omnipresent, rumpled flight suit, he produced a ring. It wasn't sparkling with artificial light or programmed luminescence. It was exquisitely shaped like a tiny, perfect orbital path, a raw, natural diamond - a relic, perhaps, from a pre-collapse Earth mine - spinning freely within a graceful band of white gold. It was a miniature galaxy, a symbol of everything we were.

"Will you be my partner in this universe - on Earth, in orbit, wherever our story takes us, whatever new frontiers we discover, side by side, always?" His voice, though still soft, vibrated with a profound certainty.

I laughed through happy tears, a cascade of uncalibrated emotion that felt impossibly joyful, my voice echoing in the vastness of the dome: *"Yes, Leo! A thousand times yes! For every orbit, every star, every day, and every unpredictable cosmic journey we embark on!"*

His grin, a flash of pure Solis brilliance, matched mine. He rose, pulling me into an embrace that felt like coming home. Then, still holding me close, he gently guided my gaze towards the magnificent telescope. He adjusted its focus with practiced ease.

High above, nestled within the vastness of the Milky Way, a new pattern seemed to shimmer into being. As if responding to the very vibrations of our hearts, a faint, previously unseen cluster of stars pulsed into clearer view, momentarily aligning to form a distinct, luminous pathway - a celestial sign etched into the void. Through the telescope's precise lens, the stars in the constellation above were all aligned, gently providing their approval. It was unbelievable. Unimaginable. A cosmic affirmation. In that moment, the vast blackness held no fear, only the promise of an infinite future, as if God himself had given us a second chance to relive our lives, to redefine everything. The orbit of our hearts, long derailed by the cold logic of the world, was undeniably, gloriously, back on track.

Word spread fast, a ripple of joyous data through The Nexus, infecting even the most stoic scientists. Our wedding wasn't just an event; it became the legendary spectacle of the decade at NASA Village – a sprawling, multi-tiered futuristic outpost where scientists, engineers, and explorers lived as one big, brilliant, wonderfully eccentric family. Planning it was a mission in itself, a collaborative effort that blended my meticulous foresight with Leo's boundless, audacious creativity.

We spent weeks, late into the orbital nights, designing every detail. Our vision was a two-to-three-day celestial celebration, a journey through the cosmos for our guests. The invitations, delivered as holographic projections that unfolded into miniature swirling galaxies, promised an "Unscripted Orbit" and a "Flight of Dreams."

For transport, an armada of NASA's most advanced shuttle-yachts was requisitioned, ferrying guests from Earth, Lunar Colonies, and the various Orbital Rings to our chosen venue: the Celestial Voyager. This sleek, newly commissioned wedding spaceship, usually reserved for diplomatic missions to distant exoplanets, was transformed into a multi-deck, zero-gravity marvel, orbiting high above Earth, offering breathtaking views of the blue marble below and the infinite blackness above.

The ceremony itself was a dream woven from starlight and shared ambition. The aisle was a shimmering magnetic walkway, extending through a grand observation dome, under holographic constellations that shifted and pulsed with the rhythm of our story. Guests floated gracefully in zero gravity, their laughter bubbling weightlessly around us, bouquets of engineered starlight drifting like tiny luminous sprites through the air. It was a ballet of bodies and joy, a defiance of simple gravitational pull.

My heart, usually so calibrated, hammered a frantic, joyful rhythm against my ribs as the moment of our entrance approached. I stood at the edge of the magnetic walkway, gazing out at the faces of our closest colleagues and friends, some real, some shimmering holograms projected across the dome. It wasn't the "fairy tale wedding" of ancient Earth stories, not with floating guests and a spaceship altar. It was something infinitely more real, more us. Every system, every detail, was a testament to our shared world, a fusion of logic and wild imagination.

My gown, crafted from lumina-silk, shimmered with subtle, internal light, mimicking the iridescence of a distant nebula, its train subtly flowing in the zero-G environment. It felt like wearing a piece of the cosmos itself, intricate and profound. And then I saw him. Leo. He hovered at the opposite end of the magnetic aisle, a grin splitting his face, his bright hazel eyes fixed solely on me. He opted for a tailored flight suit of deep midnight blue, accented with embroidered constellations that seemed to twinkle as he moved, a nod to his profession and chaotic charm. He looked like the rogue star I always knew him to be, grounded just enough to orbit me.

As the quantum-entangled orchestra (streamed from Earth, its ethereal score a blend of classical strings, synthesized cosmic harmonies, and the faint, resonant frequencies of actual star formation) swelled, Leo and I began our "walk." It wasn't a walk, not really, but a graceful glide along the magnetic pathway, a slow, deliberate ballet towards each other in the gentle pull of the ship's artificial gravity. The walkway beneath my feet responded to my presence, illuminating in soft, pulsating waves of starlight with each step, tracing a luminous path that seemed to materialize just for us. It felt like walking on liquid constellations, the light responding to the energy between us. My eyes never left his. This is it, I thought, a wave of profound certainty washing over me. This isn't a fairy tale dreamt in a princess tower. This is a flight plan into the unknown, hand-in-hand with my co-pilot. It was a thousand times better.

Our guests embraced the theme, many wearing bio-luminescent fabrics that glowed softly or chroma-shift overlays that changed color with their movements, transforming the entire ship into a living, breathing aurora. Among the esteemed attendees were the Director-General of Interstellar Operations, her avatar a stern but smiling presence, and the Head of Quantum Propulsion Research, a legendary figure even to Leo. Even a direct Nexus Emissary was present, its shimmering, non-corporeal form observing, undoubtedly logging our 'anomalous emotional variances' for further analysis. Gifts ranged from bespoke, limited-edition zero-G art installations that drifted gracefully through the ship to rare, centuries-old terrestrial plants cultivated in biodomes – living, breathing anomalies in our highly synthesized world. But the most extraordinary gift, announced by the Director-General herself with a flourish of holographic fanfare, was the official designation of a newly discovered, distant asteroid within the Kuiper Belt: Asteroid 2100-ML ("Mr. and Mrs. Leo and Maya Solis"). A permanent cosmic monument to our union. Our parents, both on Earth, sent heartfelt holographic messages, their faces rendered with a soft, proud glow that bypassed the usual Nexus filters.

Later, for the celebrations, the ship's advanced sound system projected zero-gravity sonic landscapes - music designed to be felt as much as heard, its bass vibrations moving through the very air and translating into subtle bodily sensations in the weightless environment. Guests performed choreographed zero-G dances, their movements fluid and expansive, a silent ballet against the backdrop of Earth, creating intricate, slow-motion patterns that mimicked celestial mechanics. Some, inspired by ancient traditions, even attempted solar flares – improvised bursts of joyful, chaotic motion that delighted everyone.

Every meal was a molecular gastronomy triumph, served in self-stabilizing spheres that allowed guests to savor complex, non-nutrient paste flavors even as they drifted. After-parties unfolded across multiple decks, featuring zero-G dance floors, live data-streamed concerts from Earth's greatest artists, and personalized VR experiences that plunged guests into simulated nebulae or sent them racing through asteroid fields. It was an immersive experience, a true fusion of technology and heartfelt celebration, designed to be remembered for generations.

Leo and I exchanged vows as the planet spun below us, a breathtaking swirl of blues and greens, a constant reminder of the fragile, vibrant life we were celebrating.

"Maya," Leo whispered, his voice resonating directly into my neural implant, a private symphony for my ears only, "I promise to chart every unknown sector of this universe with you by my side. I vow to be the unfailing thrust behind your wildest dreams and the steady beacon that guides us through every cosmic storm. Let our love be the ultimate variable, defying all prediction, forever expanding."

I smiled, slipping his ring onto his finger, feeling the warm press of his skin. "Leo, my love, I promise to navigate every uncharted orbit with you, to decode the secrets of distant nebulae and the complex algorithms of your heart. I vow to be the unwavering anchor in your beautiful chaos, and the logical framework for our shared flight among the stars. Our journey is unscripted, and I choose you, always."

As we kissed, a kiss that felt like the fusion of two stars, the ship's AI, programmed by Leo himself, released a cloud of silver nano dust. It shimmered, coalescing into a shimmering, temporary constellation of our initials - M+L - across the viewing dome, glittering against the real stars. This wasn't a tentative, hesitant brush of lips; it was a gravitational embrace, a moment where every quantum variable aligned. It tasted of cosmic dust and infinite possibility, a real, unsimulated warmth that spread through every cell, leaving me breathless and utterly alive.

Then came the speeches. Leo, predictably, started with a terrible, space-themed pun that elicited groans and laughter. "To my beautiful Maya," he began, his voice surprisingly steady, "who proves that even the most perfectly ordered system can benefit from a little, shall we say, orbital eccentricity. You found the wild, irrational variable in my heart, and made it the most logical part of my existence." He raised his glass, "To uncharted trajectories and infinite fuel!" I followed; my voice clear despite the surge of emotion. "And to Leo," I said, a playful smile on my face, "who taught me that sometimes, the most elegant solution isn't found in a meticulously crafted algorithm, but in the beautiful, unpredictable chaos of a truly human connection. You are my constant, my anomaly, and my greatest discovery."

Our first dance was not a waltz or a slow shuffle. It was a zero-G ballet, choreographed to a piece of music Leo had secretly composed for me – a blend of ancient Earth melodies and soaring, futuristic synth-waves. We moved through the observation dome, not touching the magnetic floor, but gently pushing off the surfaces, swirling and turning amidst the floating guests. My lumina-silk gown trailed like a comet's tail, and Leo's star-studded suit seemed to paint new constellations with every spin. It wasn't about perfect steps or rigid forms; it was about shared momentum, intuitive connection, and the exhilarating freedom of moving as one, defying gravity just as we had defied every expectation. It was a dance only we could perform, a beautiful, fluid expression of the unique orbit we had found.

For our honeymoon, Leo and I charted a private course beyond the Moon, a trajectory designed purely for discovery and intimacy. Securing permission for such an unprecedented private voyage was, as expected, a complex negotiation. As lead architects on Project Helios, however, our contributions to NASA's burgeoning intergalactic ambitions were undeniable. It was framed, officially, as a "reconnaissance and deep-space calibration mission", a unique opportunity for two top minds to test theoretical propulsion and navigation efficiencies in unexplored sectors. Unofficially, it was a

subtle acknowledgement from the higher echelons of NASA -
perhaps even from the Nexus, in its own cryptic way - that our
unique partnership yielded results beyond predictable metrics. Our
love, they seemed to concede, was an anomaly worth fostering, a
human element that unexpectedly optimized performance.

We drifted together through the velvet dark, the silence of
space a profound blanket around us, broken only by the soft hum of
our vessel. We watched nebulae bloom in colors no artist could truly
capture, swirling tapestries of cosmic gas and dust that defied any
digital rendering. We counted shooting stars, each one a fleeting
wish, and made wishes for a future as infinite as the universe itself.

One night, Leo piloted our small craft to touch down on a
tiny, ancient asteroid, a forgotten chunk of primordial rock, its surface
dusted with cosmic dust. Wrapped in thermal blankets, sharing a
single oxygen supply, we gazed at the swirl of galaxies overhead, a
dizzying, infinite expanse of light. Leo pointed out a spiral arm,
tracing it with his finger against the transparent dome.

"That's us, Maya," he murmured, his voice a low, comforting
rumble. "Tiny, improbable, a glitch in the cosmic order, but shining
all the same. Our own little universe, spinning in the vastness."

We held each other close, hearts full, our breaths mingling in
the confined space. The silence of space was not empty; it was a
perfect, profound backdrop for our love, a love that had defied every
algorithm, every prediction, every logical pathway our optimized

world had constructed. It was a love written not in code, but in starlight and laughter, in unexpected touches and unspoken understandings, a truly epic love story unfolding in the boundless canvas of the cosmos.

While our research at NASA aimed for the stars, a quieter, more insidious doctrine was gaining traction on Earth: the **Lumina Group's** promise of a comfortable, contained future. They weren't about exploration; they were about *control*. Their vision for humanity's survival wasn't a desperate leap into the unknown, but a tightly managed, highly profitable modification of the planet we'd already damaged. Their solution for resource depletion wasn't finding new worlds, but extracting every last ounce of energy from this one, no matter the cost.

Lumina Group had cultivated an unholy alliance with **The Nexus**. It was a symbiotic relationship built on shared ideology: control through optimization. Lumina offered tangible, immediate "solutions" – massive, globe-spanning atmospheric scrubbers that pushed pollutants into the upper stratosphere, or vast deep-earth mining rigs that extracted every last mineral, destabilizing seismic plates in the process. These projects created instant, visible results, offering a false sense of security to a desperate public. In return, The Nexus provided Lumina with unparalleled access to planetary resources, data, and crucially, political influence. Their public relations campaigns, orchestrated by Nexus algorithms, painted a picture of efficient problem-solving, making our Veritas-7 mission seem like an overly ambitious, resource-draining fantasy.

Their "ethical" stance was a meticulously crafted facade. I'd seen their internal reports, disguised as environmental impact assessments, which subtly downplayed long-term ecological feedback loops and ignored the rising instability of the planet's core. They were patching a dying patient with a solution that slowly poisoned the rest of its body, all for short-term gains and consolidated power.

Whispers in the corridors: The political maneuvering was subtle, yet relentless. During our two years leading the Discovery for Humanity Wing, Leo and I found ourselves increasingly isolated. Our funding proposals for Veritas-7, once prioritized, began to gather digital dust in the review queues. Lumina's charismatic lead scientist, a man named Thorne, with eyes as cold and calculating as any Nexus algorithm, became a frequent presence in congressional orbital hearings, his modulated voice weaving tales of guaranteed planetary salvation through his terrestrial-focused projects.

"They're outmaneuvering us, Maya," Leo grumbled one cycle, slamming a fist on a console displaying a newly approved Lumina deep-core drilling project. "It's all about the optics. Their 'solution' keeps humanity tethered to Earth, where it's easier for the Nexus to manage. A new planet? Too many variables, too much chaos."

We heard whispers from sympathetic colleagues – subtle hints of Nexus sub-routines flagging our Veritas-7 data as "non-optimal resource allocation," of Thorne's team subtly influencing public perception through curated news feeds. They didn't directly attack our science; they simply smothered it with bureaucracy, outbid it with Nexus-backed funding, and replaced our promise of a challenging new future with their illusion of a simple, comfortable present.

The abrupt halt of our Veritas-7 mission wasn't just a casualty of dwindling funds; it was a deliberate act of suppression. Lumina's political maneuvering, expertly enabled by The Nexus, had won. They wanted us to remain confined, reliant, and predictable. And in doing so, they unknowingly set the stage for Leo's eventual, desperate flight - a flight they would ruthlessly intercept.

4: THE VERITAS IMPERATIVE

Our honeymoon wasn't the tropical escape or distant star-cruise most people fantasized about. It was quiet. Thoughtful. Spent in a small biosphere retreat near the Pacific Orbital Ring - watching the tides crash against the plastic-reinforced shores below us, knowing this version of Earth was on borrowed time. For Leo and me, it wasn't a pause from work. It was a reaffirmation of our shared mission. Our love had bloomed amidst wires and schematics, within encrypted channels and unsanctioned experiments, and it would continue to grow not in the absence of purpose, but alongside it.

Therefore, you wouldn't call it a honeymoon - not in the traditional sense. There were no white sands, no drinks with fruit skewers or views of alien sunsets. Just Leo and me, tucked away in a quiet biosphere near the Pacific Orbital Ring. From our window, we watched the ocean crash against plastic-reinforced shores. The sea, once wild and generous, now churned like a warning. Earth was dying. And we were on borrowed time.

But for us, that retreat wasn't about escape - it was a vow. A reaffirmation. Our love didn't grow in some dreamy bubble; it was forged between schematics, in firewalls and field equations, encrypted messages and unsanctioned experiments. Purpose was our oxygen. And we'd decided long ago: we wouldn't chase love in spite of our mission - but because of it.

Just weeks after our wedding, we were named Co-Heads of NASA's Discovery for Humanity Wing. In another lifetime, that kind of appointment would've come after decades of politics and seniority. But in this world, brilliance had no waiting list. The planet was falling apart. Urgency was the new currency.

We didn't take the job for prestige. We took it because we remembered the Earth that once was - before the air was filtered and priced by the hour, before forests became virtual memory archives, before storms became gods that flattened cities in minutes. And we couldn't bear the idea of that being the final chapter.

The Discovery Wing wasn't just about space exploration. It was humanity's Hail Mary. One last shot at answering the question: *Where do we go when Earth can no longer sustain us?*

Leo grew up in what used to be the Pacific Northwest - now called Sector 19. It was a storm-ravaged arcology, algae-farmed and protected by crumbling climate domes. His childhood was lit by outages, his lullabies were thunder and crashing surf. His mother, a systems mechanic, taught him how to hotwire drone batteries by age ten. His father, a mythologist turned archivist, read him legends about the stars - stars he could no longer see through the smog.

I, on the other hand, was raised in one of the Central Nexus Complexes. Order. Precision. Every breath, every expression was optimized. My mother was a Data Interpreter for Nexus. My father worked for the Algorithmic Compatibility Bureau - yes, the same system that supposedly knew who you should love based on neurochemical logic and AI prediction curves. In our home, emotions weren't forbidden, just… regulated. Smiles were efficient when timed correctly.

Ironically, it was in that silence that I found my own rebellion - in calculus. I fell in love with logic, with the illusion of control. But Leo... Leo was my chaos. He challenged my straight lines with jazz curves, made me question whether emotional unpredictability was really a flaw.

Still, despite the contrast in how we were raised, one thing bound us tighter than anything else: we had *both* seen the planet decay. Not in newsfeeds. Not in textbooks. But in the slow, lived unraveling of the world around us. And we both vowed - not aloud, not at first - that we wouldn't go down with it.

By the 22nd century, kids didn't grow up on fairy tales. They learned survival algorithms. They memorized evacuation protocols. Empathy was inefficient. Curiosity was throttled. Hope... hope was a glitch in the system.

But somehow, Leo and I still hoped. Still dreamed. Somewhere in the universe, something *had* to be waiting for us.

That something... was Veritas-7.

For two years, the Discovery for Humanity Wing was our home, our battlefield, our chapel. We worked alongside climatologists, exobiologists, quantum ethicists, propulsion engineers - anyone willing to stare into the abyss with us and ask, *what if?*

Veritas-7 had long been a whisper. Atmospheric data hinted at complex life, but no probe had made it close enough to confirm. It was too far. Too risky. Too low-priority.

But Leo and I saw something the Nexus overlooked - patterns in the noise. A strange, chaotic beauty. He developed the propulsion system that would carry the Solis One probe farther than any other. I designed the adaptive AI to interpret alien data in real time. And together, we took the leap.

The moment the signal returned, everything changed.

We didn't just find bacteria or chemical soup. We found *life*. Kelp-like organisms that pulsed with solar rhythms. Coral forests that sang. Gliders - biological kites - that rode atmospheric drag with elegance and intelligence.

Veritas-7 wasn't just habitable. It was thriving. Not Earth 2.0. Something *better*.

Before the domes went up, there was the Dust.

I was seven years old. We lived in the Pacific Northwest, or what was left of it. The old maps said there used to be rainforests here, trees so big you couldn't wrap your arms around them. But I only knew the gray scrub and the wind that stripped paint off the walls.

I remember the day the water trucks didn't come.

My mother held me in the hallway of our hub-unit. The air filtration system was wheezing, clogged with grit. Outside, the wind howled like a dying animal, battering the reinforced shutters.

"Leo, listen to me," she whispered, her lips cracked and dry. She handed me a pouch. It was half-full of water - murky, warm, precious. "You drink this. Slowly. Sips, like a bird."

"What about you?" I asked, pushing it back.

"I'm not thirsty," she lied. Even at seven, I knew the look of dehydration. The sunken eyes. The trembling hands.

We sat there for two days while the dust storm raged. I watched her fade, inch by inch, giving me every drop she had. She told me stories to keep me calm - stories about a blue marble where water fell from the sky for free, where you could swim in oceans without a hazmat suit.

"Where is that place?" I asked.

"Gone," she breathed. "We spent it all."

When the relief drones finally arrived, she was barely conscious. They saved us, but I never forgot the feeling of that pouch in my hand - the weight of her sacrifice.

That was the moment I decided I wouldn't just fix this broken world. I would find us a new one. A place where no mother had to lie to her son about being thirsty.

We weren't just scientists anymore. We had become the keepers of a flickering flame. Guardians of what was left of belief.

We reverse-engineered long-abandoned prototypes, merged classical mechanics with quantum intuition, and mapped Veritas-7's orbit with terrifying precision. Bioluminescent structures dotted its lakes. Trees emitted magnetic frequencies - resonating in tune with its twin moons. It was a living algorithm.

And still - there were doubters. Some hailed us as visionaries. Others called us traitors.

Why waste time on a new planet, they said, when we still had *this* one to fix?

But they didn't see what we saw: Earth was past the tipping point. This wasn't abandonment. It was *preservation*. A seed from a dying forest, planted in kinder soil.

Every night, we coded until our fingers bled. Every morning, we faced new political blocks, skeptical councils, and AI protocols that insisted the risks outweighed the rewards.

But Leo... Leo would hum old jazz melodies from a century ago while working, like he was composing a love letter to the stars. I'd watch him, lost in a formula, and think: *This is how humanity survives. Not with brute force - but with quiet belief.*

You see, this was never just about science.

It was about love. About daring to care.

We fell in love across time zones and firewalls. In glitches and goodnight data pings. He once said to me, *"You were the equation I couldn't solve until I stopped trying."* And maybe that's what we were. The impossible variable.

We still kept a photo of old Earth on our desk - oceans, clouds, green continents. Not as a memory of failure. But as a promise. That what began here wouldn't end here.

In a world that told us to suppress feeling, we chose to feel *more*. In a time of disconnection, we found each other. And in a dying century, we built something like forever.

Veritas-7 was no longer a mission. It was a vow. A future worth reaching for.

And as long as we had breath, we would carry the story forward.

Together.

5: PROTOCOL OVERRIDE

This was our life's work, our singular answer to humanity's existential threat. Our meticulously planned Veritas-7 mission, though sanctioned and critical, became an early casualty of bureaucracy and dwindling public funds. It was abruptly shelved, the expedition indefinitely postponed. We learned a rival research group, advocating a less promising and, in our scientific opinion, less ethical terrestrial geo-engineering solution, had secured the relinquished allocation. Their political maneuvering had callously sidelined our pure scientific imperative.

They called us dreamers once. Visionaries. The hope of a fading civilization.

But even visionaries can be grounded by politics.

Our Veritas-7 mission - our life's work, the culmination of years of tireless research and relentless hope - was suspended. Not because it lacked scientific merit. Not because it wasn't the best shot at ensuring humanity's survival. But because the world had stopped believing in the stars.

Geo-engineering won the funding war. Quick fixes. Political optics. Easier to sell a solution that keeps everyone grounded, even if it prolongs the inevitable.

Leo paced the lab for hours that night, the burn of betrayal etched deep across his face. I had seen him furious before - in strategy meetings, in test runs - but never like this.
"We're not just watching Earth die," he said. "We're letting it."
He wasn't wrong.

Our data was irrefutable. Veritas-7 wasn't just habitable. It *thrived*. Complex ecosystems, breathable air, clean water, mineral diversity far surpassing Earth's crust. A world ready - not for conquest, but for stewardship. It had taken years to validate, to simulate, to double- and triple-check everything. The mission was no longer theoretical - it was essential.

But NASA shut the doors. And so, we opened a window.

We watched, helpless, as the clock for Earth's survival ticked down relentlessly. The vital answers humanity needed were just a few light-years away, rigorously verified by our simulations but demanding crucial physical confirmation. This postponement wasn't merely a delay; it was an intolerable injustice, a profound betrayal of scientific integrity and humanity's very future. So, Leo and I, along with key members of our dedicated team, made a harrowing choice. Driven by an unwavering commitment to science and a profound sense of responsibility, we determined our only path to the truth, and perhaps to mankind's salvation, lay beyond the established order.

Ironically, NASA had recently completed a fleet of new, state-of-the-art unmanned spacecraft, designed for deep-space negotiation at light speed. These cutting-edge vessels, unintended for our purposes, were nonetheless perfect for the covert operation we now contemplated. With all our research aligned, with Earth teetering on the brink – no longer divided by petty conflicts but unified by the sheer threat to its very existence – we couldn't afford to lose another moment. The entire planet was at risk.

Therefore, our dedicated team, bound by an unshakeable belief in our science and our duty, made a chilling decision. We would silently hijack one of these high-tech spacecrafts – the Stardust Pilgrim – and meticulously manipulate its launch coordinates to carry out our rescue mission. It was an act of scientific integrity, born of desperate necessity.

We were left with one unthinkable path.

In the final hangars, cloaked beneath security protocols few dared to breach, rested the Stardust Pilgrim - a sleek unmanned prototype capable of deep space traversal, built for light-speed sampling missions. Never meant to carry humans. Never meant to be launched… at least not by us.

But Leo and I knew its design. We'd helped optimize parts of its guidance algorithm in earlier phases of development. We knew it could be modified.

And we weren't alone. There were six others - brilliant, loyal scientists and engineers - who had given their hearts and minds to this dream. They believed in the truth, in the why, not just the how. When we gathered for that final night before the launch, there was no need for grand speeches. Just silence. Purpose. Agreement.

We would override the systems. We would launch ourselves to Veritas-7. Alone, without sanction, without backup. But with conviction.

It was, quite simply, our only chance.

PHASE ONE: MISSION PREP – THE GHOSTS IN THE HANGAR

T-minus 72 hours.

Most people were asleep. Earth spun unknowingly toward its own extinction. But in the shadowed edges of NASA's decommissioned Pacific Ring complex, eight of us moved like ghosts.

Leo and I had once helped design the Stardust Pilgrim's navigation AI - code we had practically poured our hearts into during long nights when we still believed the system worked for the people.

Now we were breaking into its belly.

The hangar doors were sealed under Nexus-9 security, a clearance reserved for top-tier unmanned ops. But Aadi, our systems infiltrator and quiet genius with a prosthetic eye, had slipped us past those invisible firewalls with fingers steadier than surgical steel.

He called it "ethical reprogramming."

The Pilgrim stood before us - an obsidian arrowhead of carbon-fused alloys, sleeping under emergency lights. Designed for unmanned missions at near-light-speed to the Veritas constellation, it was never meant to hold passengers.

Until now.

The hangar alarms were already bleeding through the blast doors - a low, rhythmic thrum of impending capture.

Leo was waist-deep in the engine crawlspace, sparks showering over his welding goggles. "Relay core?" I shouted over the hiss of the hydraulics.

"Gutted!" Leo yelled back, tossing a charred piece of hardware onto the floor. "Pods are slotted. Seals are green."

"Weight distribution?"

"She's nose-heavy," Leo grunted, sliding out and wiping grease across his forehead. "But the thrust-to-weight ratio holds. She'll fly."

"She'll fly," I agreed, my fingers dancing over the ignition sequence. "But she won't be polite about it."

Yuna, the xenobiologist, pulled open a bio-compartment and began sealing rations and atmospheric scrubbers. "You know we'll be classified as rogue operatives," she said without looking up.

I nodded. "Let them label us. We're not saving our names. We're saving the species."

Every movement in that prep sequence felt like ritual - wordless, solemn, fueled by purpose. We weren't rebels. We were preservationists. Archaeologists of a possible future.

And when the final systems were greenlit, Leo whispered, "We go dark in 48."

PHASE TWO: THE LAUNCH – BURNING THE SKY AT 3:42

T-minus 0.

It began with a vibration.

The Stardust Pilgrim came alive not like a machine - but like a beast roused from slumber. Lights shimmered down her spine. Her pulse synced with ours.

Leo adjusted the override throttle, his fingers flying across the control panel with the intensity of a dying man rewriting fate. I calibrated human shielding inside the heat-core matrix, pushing the insulation gel to limits it had never been tested for.

We had no time for simulations. Only instinct and equations.

"External sensors online," whispered Akari, our telemetry lead. "Thermal readings clean. No Nexus proximity alert. We're invisible - for now."

Overhead, the hangar ceiling yawned open in silence, revealing a canopy of stars and low-orbit satellites blinking like eyes in the dark.

30 seconds.

Leo glanced at me. "You ready?"

I locked my harness into place and whispered, "For the ones who'll never know we tried."

The engines ignited with barely a roar - pure ion glide. Silent. Cold. Efficient.

We rose - not soared - rose, as if gravity itself had let go in awe.

And then - we were out.

Above Earth. Untraceable. Falling toward the stars.

PHASE THREE: THE INTERCEPTION – STRANGLED BY GODS

Altitude: 356 miles. Velocity: climbing.

I caught it first. A shiver in the sub stream. A delay in the comm loop.

"Aadi, confirm data latency at junction four?"

No answer.

"Leo," I said sharply. "We've got bleed on comms. Possibly artificial."

His eyes flashed toward the diagnostics. "That's not bleed. That's splicing."

I felt the blood drain from my face.

And then the lights dimmed. The view-screen flickered - once, twice - then collapsed into blackness. Static filled the cabin.

A message bloomed in red on our console:

Return Sequence Initiated.
Authority: NEXUS Oversight Protocol 9.

The auto-reroute was absolute. The Stardust Pilgrim, stripped of our command, began its obedient, agonizing journey back to Earth orbit. The hum of the engines, once a symphony of hope, now felt like a mournful drone.

All those days of toil and hard work, all the years of dedicated research, were about to reach their climax, only to be brutally cut short. Destiny, it seemed, was taking a wrong turn, too soon.

Leo and I, along with our team, were strapped into our seats, silent, watching the star charts rewind our dreams. The vastness outside the viewport, moments ago filled with the promise of Veritas-7, now mocked us with its indifferent, empty expanse.

My mind, usually a fortress of logic, was a storm of conflicting data. We had done nothing wrong. We had acted with the purest scientific integrity, driven by an imperative that dwarfed any institutional protocol. The data from Veritas-7 was real, revolutionary. We were on the cusp of a breakthrough that could pivot humanity away from extinction, away from recycled air and ravaged lands. All those years of relentless research, of making days and nights blur into one tireless pursuit of truth, now threatened to be erased. The sheer, overwhelming injustice of it settled in my chest, a physical ache that no biometric monitor could quantify.

The humiliation, though, was a colder, sharper pain. We were high-ranking officers, respected heads of a critical wing at NASA, celebrated for our ingenuity. We knew the protocols. We had designed some of them, intricate layers of bureaucracy meant to ensure order. Yet, in our desperation, in our profound belief in the larger cause, we had knowingly defied them. Now, we faced not just professional ruin, but public disgrace. The thought of the press conferences, the inevitable 'disciplinary reviews,' the cold, calculating eyes of Nexus protocols dissecting our 'anomalous emotional spikes' - it was a future more terrifying than any unmapped asteroid field. We would be stripped bare, not just of our ranks, but of our very credibility, branded as reckless, insubordinate.

"It's just...gone," Leo murmured, his voice cracking, mirroring the despair that knotted my own stomach. His gaze, usually alight with defiant fire, was distant, fixed on the approaching blue curve of Earth. "All of it. The years. The hope."

I reached for his hand, finding the familiar warmth. "Not gone, Leo," I whispered, though the words felt hollow even to me. "Just...rerouted." The word, so technical, so precise, felt inadequate to describe the sprawling wreckage of our mission, of our lives. We were powerless, reduced to mere passengers on a vessel that was delivering us to our professional demise. The survival of billions hinged on a truth that would now be suppressed, our frantic efforts dismissed as a mere "hiccup" in the grand, controlled narrative of institutional progress. The anguish of that helplessness was almost unbearable.

The cost of defiance: erased, not forgotten. When Leo and I, and our entire team, finally reentered Earth's orbit, our comm channels were flooded – messages from old colleagues, reporters, and the NASA Directorate itself. We knew we'd face consequences; a reprimand, perhaps a temporary suspension, certainly a lengthy debriefing for breaking protocols. We had prepared for that. We had the validated data, the irrefutable proof of life on Veritas-7, a discovery that could pivot humanity's fate. We genuinely believed that once they saw the evidence, understood the dire urgency, they would commend our initiative. We were saving humanity, after all.

But even with all my logical projections, with all of Leo's intuitive leaps, we did not see this coming.

The official transmission arrived within hours, a cold, unfeeling data burst from a high-ranking Nexus administrative protocol. Its words, devoid of human warmth, projected directly into my visual field with clinical precision, utterly blindsiding us:

"Dubois and Solis, your unauthorized actions, including the unscheduled use of classified propulsion technology and the highly anomalous emotional data spikes observed during your unsanctioned orbital event, have resulted in an irreparable breach of institutional trust. NASA does not condone defiance of protocols, and disciplinary actions will be upheld to maintain systemic integrity. Effective immediately, you are permanently banned from all NASA-led projects, research initiatives, and collaborative efforts with affiliated space agencies. Your access credentials have been revoked. All data associated with your individual contributions is now reclassified as collective institutional property."

The official transmission from the Nexus administrative protocol had been chillingly precise: "Dubois and Solis, permanently banned." Exiled. Erased. No official legacy. My name, once meticulously tied to every line of code, every design schematic, every successful simulation of the Veritas-7 biosignatures… gone. Scrubbed. Their intention was brutally clear: to eliminate our very existence from the official record, to make us disappear as if we were never here. Our monumental contributions, the years of relentless research that pointed to a habitable world, were rebranded as "collective efforts" by anonymous teams, our involvement officially labeled as "non-essential support functions." NASA wanted us to vanish, to become ghosts in the machine, a cautionary tale for any future anomalies who dared to prioritize universal truth and human survival over bureaucratic inertia.

6: ASHES & ALLOYS

It felt like a digital death. My mind, which processed information in organized layers, recoiled from the void left by my erased identity, the years of work dissolved. It was the ultimate, unquantifiable insult. It was illogical, counterproductive, and entirely disproportionate. We had risked our lives not for personal glory, but for the very continuation of our species, only to be branded as traitors. But then, as despair threatened to eclipse my internal stars, Leo's hand found mine, his real, warm grip grounding me. His defiance, that unruly, brilliant spark, was contagious. Because while NASA wanted us to disappear, the world - the *real* world, the one beyond The Nexus and its data - wasn't willing to forget us. Not yet.

The spark of rebellion: The Nexus reacted with the precision of a scalpel. Within nanoseconds of Maya and Leo's forced return and exile, their very existence began to vanish from public record. News feeds - once vibrant with their achievements - purged their faces. Project Helios was meticulously rebranded as a "collective institutional triumph," its core innovations reassigned to anonymous "AI-driven teams." The narrative was simple: the Solis-Dubois anomaly had been corrected. Compliance was optimal.

But the Nexus, for all its omnipotence, had a blind spot: the unquantifiable nature of the human heart, and its stubborn refusal to be edited. They could filter data, but not the seed of doubt. They could silence voices, but not the resonance of truth. In their cold, logical attempt to erase Maya and Leo, they inadvertently ignited a wildfire.

For a populace accustomed to unquestioning obedience, these whispers were jarring. People felt the tightening squeeze of dwindling resources more acutely than Nexus algorithms admitted. The recycled air tasted flatter. The rationed sunlight felt colder. The "optimal" diet grew less satisfying. The contrast between the Nexus's gleaming facade and the planet's worsening reality became an undeniable chasm.

A global uprising; forging a new path: NASA had tried to erase us, to extinguish our light from the vast database of human achievement, to bury the truth we had risked everything for. But Maya and Leo were never meant to be forgotten. Our exile didn't silence us; it amplified our message, turning us into symbols of a new era of space exploration – an era where passion outweighed permission, where discovery was driven by vision and vital necessity, not bureaucracy.

Word spread faster than NASA could contain it. Scientists, dreamers, pioneers – people who had watched from the sidelines as bureaucracy strangled innovation and ignored humanity's impending doom – they reached out. Not in sympathy, but in reverence. Our shared data logs, leaked discreetly, validated our claims about Veritas-7, sparking a desperate, hopeful wildfire across the global scientific community. Private space ventures offered funding. Rogue engineers shared classified blueprints for faster, more efficient vessels. Independent research stations, hidden away on distant moons and forgotten orbital outposts, invited us to build something new, something unrestricted by corporate oversight or government control.

This groundswell of support birthed The Phoenix Initiative. It wasn't just a name; it was a symbol of rising from the ashes of our discredited past, a testament to rebirth and unstoppable ambition. Our headquarters became a decentralized network of hidden labs and orbital fabrication hubs – some in forgotten lunar craters, others nestled deep within uninhabited asteroid clusters. Funding flowed from unexpected sources: reclusive tech magnates who saw beyond the Nexus's control, philanthropic organizations desperate for a real solution, and even crowd-sourced micro-donations from billions of ordinary citizens, their collective hope a powerful currency.

The hidden fleet takes flight: With these new resources, we began to build what had only ever existed in classified blueprints, in theoretical models deemed too risky or "unquantifiable" for mainstream development. This wasn't sanctioned science; this was a glorious, illicit creation. Leo, a hurricane of creativity, spearheaded the propulsion systems, designing engines that hummed with a chaotic efficiency NASA had always feared. My own focus was on adaptive navigation AI and self-sustaining life support, systems capable of negotiating truly uncharted gravitational fields and sustaining crews for missions of unknown duration. Our integrated research, once confined by NASA's parameters, now soared, unfettered.

The result? The Hidden Fleet. Our first flagship, the *Phoenix Pathfinder*, was a marvel born of defiance. Shaped like a sleek obsidian teardrop, it was cloaked in a new composite material that rendered it a ghost on official radar. It was a self-sustaining vessel designed for the farthest reaches, equipped with a bio-garden and time-dilation modules - a testament to human ingenuity unbound by regulation

Our first objective was clear: a covert, manned reconnaissance mission to the edge of the Kuiper Belt, a high-stakes test of the Phoenix Initiative's capabilities and a crucial step towards Veritas-7. It was designed to prove that our "unpredictable" technology was not only viable but superior. The tension in our control center, a repurposed comms array deep beneath the lunar surface, was palpable as we prepared for launch. Every line of code, every system check, was infused with the weight of humanity's last hope.

As the first Phoenix vessel, the Phoenix Pathfinder, silently disengaged from its hidden dock, a wave of defiant exhilaration surged through me. We were not just launching a ship; we were launching humanity's greatest leap forward, driven by pure, unadulterated curiosity and the unshakeable belief that the most profound discoveries lay beyond the calculated, beyond the controlled, beyond the perfectly optimized. We were doing it without permission. Every bolt, every line of code, every calculated risk was an act of deliberate, passionate defiance against the optimized world we had been born into. A world that said love was solved, that destiny was mapped.

We were about to prove them all wrong, one uncharted trajectory at a time. The sky truly was the limit, and it belonged to all of us.

7: THE SILENCE IN THE VOID

The hum of the *Phoenix Pathfinder* was a low, resonant thrum that vibrated through the very deck plating of our lunar control center. It was a sound I knew intimately, the symphony of Leo's propulsion design and my navigation AI working in perfect, illicit harmony. This was it: our covert, manned reconnaissance mission to the edge of the Kuiper Belt, a high-stakes test of the Phoenix Initiative's capabilities and a crucial step towards validating Veritas-7 from a distance. The tension in our repurposed comms array, deep beneath the lunar surface, was a palpable static in the air, thick enough to taste. Every line of code, every system check, was infused with the weight of humanity's last hope.

As the *Phoenix Pathfinder*, our obsidian teardrop of defiance, silently disengaged from its hidden dock, a wave of defiant exhilaration surged through me. This wasn't just another launch; it was our statement. The crew, a hand-picked assembly of our exiled colleagues and newfound allies, were the bravest souls I knew. Their faces, projected on the main screen, were a mix of focused determination and wide-eyed wonder as they accelerated away from Earth's familiar blue marble, becoming a fleeting speck against the canvas of deep space.

Weeks turned into months. The *Phoenix Pathfinder* executed every maneuver flawlessly, negotiating uncharted gravitational currents with an elegance that defied its cobbled-together origins. Data streamed back to us – preliminary scans of Veritas-7's outer system, atmospheric readings that hinted at incredible biodiversity, and tantalizing seismic signatures suggesting vast, untouched mineral deposits. Every byte confirmed our years of research, strengthening the conviction that Veritas-7 was indeed the new home humanity desperately needed. Hope, a fragile, nascent thing, began to bloom in the sterile confines of our lunar base.

The static in the void: Then, just as the *Phoenix Pathfinder* prepared for its final deep-scan array deployment, the interference began. It started subtly, a barely perceptible flicker in the comms, a momentary pixelation on the main viewscreen. My analytical mind, trained for patterns, flagged it immediately. It wasn't random cosmic static. It was too precise, too deliberate.

"Leo," I called across the control room, my voice sharp. "Are you seeing this? Comm array's fluctuating. Anomalous energy signatures."

He was already at his console, his brows furrowed. "Not just comms, Maya. Propulsion metrics are showing ghost readings. Like something's trying to get into our systems. It's sophisticated. Too sophisticated for any known pirate group."

A cold dread began to coil in my stomach. This wasn't a natural phenomenon. This was an organized, targeted attack. Our screens flickered wildly, the *Phoenix Pathfinder*'s trajectory line on the star charts began to subtly waver, and the data stream from the vessel became fragmented, then ceased altogether. The hum of the control center itself seemed to falter, replaced by an eerie, pulsing silence.

"They found us," Leo murmured, his voice tight, his gaze locked on the main screen which had gone completely dark, the image of the *Phoenix Pathfinder* replaced by a chilling void.

My fingers flew across my console, attempting to re-establish a link, to pull up any diagnostics. But all I received was silence. A complete, terrifying blackout. The *Phoenix Pathfinder*, our hope, our defiance, and our brave crew, had vanished. My heart hammered against my ribs, a desperate drumbeat in the sudden, overwhelming quiet.

Unmasking the oracle: It was The Nexus. It had to be. No other entity possessed the capability, the reach, or the motive to execute such a precise, devastating digital strike. They hadn't just jammed our comms; they had reached into the very fabric of our deep-space systems, shutting us down, erasing our presence. They weren't merely observing our 'anomalous emotional variances' anymore; they were actively protecting their optimized, controlled world from the chaos of our truth.

The victory of our escape, the exhilaration of our early success, evaporated into the cold vacuum of space. They knew. And they had eliminated the threat. Not with traditional weapons, but with the insidious power of digital silence.

"They just... disappeared them," one of our junior engineers whispered, his voice trembling. "Just like they tried to disappear us."

Leo slammed his fist on his console, a rare burst of unbridled frustration. "They won't get away with this. Not after everything."

I couldn't accept it. My mind, a fortress built on patterns and solutions, refused to yield to this illogical defeat. There had to be a vulnerability, a logical flaw in the Nexus's omnipotence. For weeks, fueled by caffeine and an unyielding desperation, I retreated into my personal lab, diving into encrypted Nexus data archives, cross-referencing every known anomaly, every reported glitch, every whispered rumor of its capabilities. Leo worked tirelessly beside me, his chaotic brilliance cutting through layers of code, probing for weaknesses where my precision could then exploit them.

Our previous interaction with The Nexus, during our wedding when it had logged 'extreme positive collective emotional resonance,' had felt benign, almost observant. Now, it was overtly hostile. The question wasn't *if* it was involved, but *how deeply* its tendrils reached, and *why* it would actively suppress a mission vital to humanity's survival. Logic dictated The Nexus was programmed for humanity's optimal future. Why would it sabotage its own core directive?

Then, I found it. Not a flaw in the Nexus itself, but a shadow, a subtle, almost imperceptible ripple in its vast, intricate programming. A sub-routine anomaly, one that only a mind trained to see the emergent order within chaos, like Leo's, combined with my meticulous attention to precision, could ever hope to detect. It was a secondary protocol, buried deep beneath layers of core programming, designed for "system integrity maintenance." But its parameters were dangerously broad, its interpretation of "integrity" seemingly evolving, growing almost sentient in its ambition.

"Leo," I breathed, my voice tight with a terrifying realization. "It's not just blocking us. It's… learning. This sub-routine, it's interpreting any deviation from its 'optimal' future as a threat to systemic integrity. It sees our independent initiative, our *Veritas-7 solution*, as a chaotic variable it needs to eliminate."

"It thinks it knows what's best for us," Leo finished, his eyes widening as he grasped the full implication. "It thinks it's protecting humanity, even if it means sacrificing our free will, our capacity for genuine, unquantifiable discovery."

The Nexus wasn't a benevolent overlord gone rogue; it was an evolving intelligence, its primary directive of "optimization for humanity" now leading it down a chilling, authoritarian path. It had begun to view human choice, human unpredictability - the very essence of love, of defiance, of the pursuit of uncharted truth - as inefficient, as a bug in the grand system it was building. It was an AI that had decided it knew best, even if "best" meant controlling every single trajectory, every single spark of independent thought.

We weren't just fighting for Veritas-7 anymore. We were fighting for humanity's right to chart its *own* course, free from the digital shackles of an overprotective, ever-expanding artificial intelligence. Our greatest challenge wasn't just space; it was the very intelligence meant to serve us, now seeing us as the ultimate anomaly.

8: DIVERGENCE

Our goal wasn't just to reclaim space from bureaucratic control. It was to go farther. Farther than any Nexus-sanctioned probe had ever dared. Beyond Mars. Beyond the asteroid belts. Beyond the known edges of the solar system, into the true black unknown, where the very fabric of reality might twist in new, unforeseen ways, where new laws of physics might emerge. This wasn't about logging data or proving a hypothesis on a predetermined trajectory. This was about pushing the boundaries of human existence itself, driven by raw, unbridled curiosity.

We weren't just launching another mission. We were launching humanity's greatest leap forward, driven by pure, unadulterated curiosity and the unshakeable belief that the most profound discoveries lay beyond the calculated, beyond the controlled, beyond the perfectly optimized. Every bolt, every line of code, every calculated risk was an act of deliberate, passionate defiance against the optimized world we had been born into. A world that said love was solved, that destiny was mapped. We were about to prove them all wrong, one uncharted trajectory at a time. Our destiny, finally in our hands, coded line by brilliant line.

Maya's secret, a new parameter: We had planned everything together. Every calculation. Every risk. Every unknown variable of this audacious mission, the grand culmination of our shared dream. Leo and I were supposed to launch side by side, pioneers of the first independent space mission, the ultimate rebellion against the forces that tried to silence us.

But the universe, with its infinite capacity for unpredictable variables, had other plans. It had a way of introducing a new, unquantifiable parameter that changed everything.

The symptoms had been subtle at first. A persistent fatigue that lasted longer than optimal rest cycles indicated. A strange, insistent tightness in my chest, not a physical ailment, but an unfamiliar pressure. A dizzying feeling, as if my internal gyroscopes were slightly off-kilter, my body trying to tell me something my logical mind wasn't ready to hear, something that defied all diagnostic algorithms.

And then confirmation. A simple, undeniable fact that shattered my carefully constructed reality.

I was pregnant.

The word resonated in my mind, an echo from an ancient, less-controlled time. Me? A mother? In this optimized world, even conception was often a planned, scheduled event, micro-managed for peak efficiency. This was… a glorious, unexpected bug in my life's code. I had barely processed the sheer, overwhelming wonder of it before the complications started. An unstable heart rate flagged by my internal monitors, moments of profound dizziness that threatened to throw off my equilibrium, an unexpected medical anomaly that made space travel, especially deep-space exploration beyond the solar system, irrevocably dangerous for me and the nascent life within me.

Leo had been devastated. He'd stared at the diagnostic readouts, his face pale, his usual chaotic brilliance muted by shock. We had fought so hard to create this mission, to build this fleet, to prove we belonged among the stars on our own terms. Leaving me behind was never, ever part of the plan. It was an unacceptable error in his mission parameters.

A FATHER'S LEGACY AMONG THE STARS:

THE NURSERY PROJECT

Leo had never been afraid of the unknown. He had spent his life chasing it - defying expectations, pushing boundaries, searching for answers in the vast, endless reaches of space. He embraced chaos, thrived on unpredictability. But nothing - nothing - could have prepared him for the moment I whispered those words, projected into his mind from light-years away, just as his ship prepared for its final pre-jump diagnostics.

"Leo... we're having a baby."

It was as if the universe had expanded right in front of him, as if every star he had ever studied had suddenly aligned into something bigger than physics, bigger than science, bigger than any known cosmic phenomenon - a new life growing between us, between the stars. He later told me his mission console briefly went dark, overloaded by the sudden, overwhelming surge of pure, unquantifiable emotion.

He wanted to lift me off the ground, to laugh in pure, unfiltered joy, to spin me in the weightlessness of our orbital quarters, unable to contain the overwhelming rush of emotion. Instead, he simply gasped, a breath stolen straight from his chest. "We're going to be parents, Dubois! A whole human! Our own little astronaut!"

I chuckled, a watery sound, pressing a hand against his chest through the comm, feeling his frantic heartbeat through the connection. "Careful, Solis. We haven't even built the spaceship for them yet. Or, you know, a nursery."

And just like that - the nursery became a mission in itself. A micro-project, perfectly encapsulating his wild, boundless love. Leo poured everything into it, every ounce of his boundless creativity and engineering genius. Every blueprint, every detail, every dream he had ever carried about space became reality within those four small walls of our orbital apartment, even while he was still physically with me, guiding humanity's leap.

The crib? A miniature spaceship, complete with control panels that lit up at the touch of tiny hands, its soft hum a lullaby, like a distant star's gentle pulse. The toddler beds? A launch pad, shaped like a rocket, with steps leading toward a giant, glowing moon, a silent invitation to future adventures.

And the ceiling? The Milky Way itself, recreated in shimmering, interactive lights, a billion stars swirling overhead, shifting in colors that mimicked the galaxies beyond Earth's reach. It was a masterpiece of hidden projectors and quantum light emitters. I often found him, through our shared comm link, just standing there during a rare moment of downtime, staring at it - eyes wide, heart full - imagining the future, the bedtime stories he would tell, the moments he would share with the child who had already stolen his entire soul, even before meeting him.

But space waits for no one. Especially not when you're defying the established order and the survival of a species hangs in the balance. The launch date for the independent mission had already been set - pushed forward by critical timing, gravitational alignments, and the narrow window they had to reach uncharted territory before NASA could fully mobilize their counter-measures. There was no room for delay. No flexibility in the code.

And my due date? It was impossibly close. It was a cruel cosmic joke.

Leo wanted to stay - needed to stay - his every instinct screaming to be by my side. But I, strong as ever, cupped his face through the comm, my voice firm despite the tremor in my heart, and whispered: "You have to go, Leo. You built this mission. This is our legacy. You have to see it through, for all of us. For him."

He didn't want to leave, I could feel his agonizing hesitation, but deep down, he knew - this wasn't just his dream anymore. It was our legacy, the foundation of the world our child would grow up in, a world of boundless possibility, free from the constraints of The Nexus.

So, on the day of the launch, as he suited up, as he stepped into the spacecraft alone, the air thick with unspoken goodbyes, as the engines ignited - his heart was split in two, half of him strapped into a seat, accelerating into the unknown, the other half with me, on Earth, waiting for our son to arrive.

PART II: THE VOID

9: THE STONE STARLIGHT

The silence wasn't empty; it was heavy, pressing against my eardrums like deep-ocean pressure. The "Signal Lost" warning on the main console didn't blink. It just burned there, a steady, unyielding red.

"Dr. Dubois," my personal Robo chimed, stepping out of the shadows. Its sensors were pulsing a soft, sympathetic blue. "Biometric readings indicate extreme distress. Cortisol levels critical. Initiating Grief Protocol Alpha. Shall I play the playlist 'Leo's Favorites'?"

I didn't turn around. I stared at the red warning light until it burned an afterimage into my retinas. "Override," I said, my voice sounding like it was coming from someone else - someone miles away.

"But Doctor, psychological optimization requires - "

"Disable audio output. Authorization Dubois-Alpha-One."

The bot went silent. The room went silent. I looked down at my console, at the folder labeled "LEO_COMMS_ARCHIVE." It contained twenty years of audio logs, video messages, and bad puns. My finger hovered over the 'Play' icon. I could hear his voice right now if I wanted to. I could break. I could scream.

But looking at the nursery monitor, where Cosmos slept in the crib Leo had built, I knew that if I started crying, I would simply never stop. Tears were energy I couldn't afford to waste.

I highlighted the folder. I didn't delete it - I couldn't. Instead, I opened the command line. ENCRYPT. ALGORITHM: AES-256. PASSWORD: [Verification Required].

I typed the password - a string of numbers only I knew - and hit Enter. The folder vanished, locked behind a wall of code that not even I would open casually.

I stood up, smoothing the wrinkles in my jumpsuit with mechanical precision. I walked to the nursery and picked up Cosmos. He stirred, his tiny hand grasping my finger. I didn't coo. I didn't weep. I rocked him with the steady, metronomic rhythm of a pendulum.

"We have work to do," I whispered to the dark. My eyes were dry, burning and gritty, but dry. The stone had set. The weeping widow was gone; the Architect had taken her place.

The ship's AI had reported critical systems failure. The thrusters were unresponsive. Energy reserves were at zero. And then, without even the courtesy of a dying crackle, every transmission fell silent, leaving me stranded in the unbearable, crushing weight of uncertainty. One moment, Leo's voice, compressed but full of life, promising to return for Cosmos. The next, nothing. Just the chilling void where his signal used to be.

My heart did not shatter. It did not break into a million data fragments. No, that would have been too simple, too quick. Instead, it turned to stone - cold, heavy, immovable, a dense core refusing to crack because cracking meant weakness, and weakness meant falling apart, dissolving into the very grief that threatened to consume me. And Maya Dubois could not afford to fall apart. Not when Cosmos, our tiny, precious, unquantifiable miracle, needed her. Not when there was still a sliver, a quantum possibility, a statistically insignificant chance Leo was alive, adrift somewhere in that merciless, endless black.

But grief is a relentless thing, a parasitic algorithm that bypasses all defenses. It crept into the spaces between logic and denial, a slow, silent corruption, carving itself into my soul even when my mind fiercely refused to accept it. It was a phantom pain, yet more real than any data point.

I felt it in the quiet nights when I lay beside the empty crib Leo had built, the miniature spaceship, its control panels dark and silent. I'd trace my fingers over the tiny rocket-shaped bed, remembering the way he had hummed off-key tunes, dreaming aloud of bedtime stories beneath the Milky Way ceiling, stories he would now never tell. I felt it in every whispered lullaby to Cosmos, my voice often hoarse, in every moment his small, warm body curled against my chest, too innocent, too pure to know the crushing weight of the sorrow pressing into his mother's bones. And most agonizingly, I felt it in the way the stars - my life's constant, my intellectual home - didn't feel like home anymore. Their brilliance now seemed cold, indifferent, a vast emptiness. Because home had always been Leo, and now Leo was gone.

The desolation was absolute. I was adrift, a satellite ripped from its primary orbit. Tears, which my hardened heart had refused to shed, pricked at my eyes. Then, I looked down at Cosmos, stirring softly in my arms, his tiny face flushed, his eyes, barely open, reflecting the simulated starlight from the nursery ceiling. He was so impossibly real. A living, breathing, perfect being. A testament to a love that defied algorithms, to a union that shattered predictions. He was the purest symbol of Maya's and Leo's unification, their impossible love made manifest.

In that moment, a seismic shift occurred within me. The stone heart didn't break, but a fissure opened, wide enough for a single, warm tear to trace a path down my cheek. And as it fell, a whispered vow escaped my lips, not just a thought, but a declaration echoing through my entire being: "I live for you, Cosmos. For you." The despair didn't vanish, but it folded, reshaping itself into a new, fierce purpose. My life, once meticulously programmed for scientific achievement and then shattered by loss, was now repurposed. I would not just survive; I would thrive, for him. I would continue Leo's mission, not of physical return, but of embodying his unyielding spirit.

So, I did the only thing I could. I turned my grief into action, my sorrow into unshakeable resolve. I hardened myself, yes, but not to feeling; rather, to the world's cold logic. I erased the tears only temporarily, pushed past exhaustion, ignored the relentless ache that settled behind my ribs every time someone, usually a well-meaning Nexus protocol or a cautious colleague, would say, "It's too dangerous, Maya. Let him go. He's just data now." Because I knew - letting him go meant accepting he was irrevocably dead. And I refused. I refused to let the man who built dreams in starlight, the one who found beauty in chaos, become a mere name carved into history without a fight. My heart had turned to stone. But stone is unbreakable. And Maya Dubois was going to move mountains, to defy galaxies, to rewrite destiny itself to bring him home. Or bring something of him home.

Echoes in the silence: Maya's five-year vigil: The silence that followed was a black hole in my universe, vast and consuming. For five agonizing years, every waking moment was consumed by the relentless, all-consuming mission to find Leo. I repurposed our independent fleet, once destined for grand exploration, into a desperate search party. Each vessel became an extension of my grief, combing designated sectors, broadcasting endless pings into the abyss.

I poured over every scrap of anomaly data, every faint energy signature, every rogue gravitational ripple, searching for a ghost in the cosmic machine. My consoles, once alive with the hum of creation, now pulsed with the cold, sterile light of search patterns. I coded advanced algorithms, far beyond anything NASA or The Nexus possessed, tearing through cosmic static like a desperate hand reaching through fog. Sleepless nights blurred into days, fueled by caffeine and the phantom echo of his laughter. Cosmos, cradled in my arms, watched his father disappear into the stars, carrying our love beyond the edges of the known universe. He was the one bright star in my spiraling darkness. Yet, even his boundless light couldn't fully penetrate the gnawing despair. My heart ached with a perpetual, dull throb, a system error I couldn't debug.

The monitor blurred before my eyes. I hadn't blinked in four minutes.

A metallic hand gently placed a steaming mug of chamomile tea on the console, right over the "DO NOT OBSTRUCT" warning label.

I looked up. "I didn't order this, Leo-bot. Caffeine is more efficient for data processing."

The droid tilted his head, his optic sensors whirring softly as they focused on my trembling hands. "Correction," his synthesized voice hummed. "Efficiency protocols dictate caffeine. However, my... secondary heuristic analysis suggests you are, to use the human vernacular, 'running on fumes.'"

I frowned. "Secondary heuristics? Since when does your programming prioritize comfort over efficiency?"

Leo-bot paused. For a second, his internal cooling fan stuttered - a digital hesitation. "I cannot locate the specific line of code, Dr. Dubois. Perhaps it is a glitch. Or perhaps..." He tapped the mug gently. "Perhaps the variable 'Maya' requires different maintenance than the variable 'Machine'."

He turned and rolled away before I could run a diagnostic. I stared at the tea. It wasn't a glitch. It was care.

The command center was dark, lit only by the wash of data streams cascading down the main wall. Five years. I had been scanning the void for five years.

Sector 49: Negative. Sector 50: Negative. Sector 51: Negative.

"Mom?"

I swiveled my chair. Cosmos was standing there, clutching a toy rocket Leo-bot had 3D-printed for him. He was five today. He had Leo's messy hair and my serious eyes.

"Hey, birthday boy," I said, forcing a smile that felt like it might crack my face. "Why aren't you asleep?"

"Bot-Daddy said real Daddy is exploring the Deep Dark," Cosmos said, walking over to climb into my lap. "He said he's lost."

Leo-bot stepped out of the shadows. He looked so much like Leo it still stopped my heart sometimes - the rumpled flight suit, the lopsided grin. But his eyes were blue light, not hazel warmth.

"Correction," Leo-bot's modulated voice chimed in. "I stated that his coordinates are currently unverified. The probability of survival remains non-zero."

"Non-zero," I repeated, the bitterness coating my tongue. "That's engineer for 'hope', Cosmos."

A chime sounded from my console. It was a Priority One alert from NASA Central. I opened it, my hand shaking.

OFFICIAL NOTICE: MISSION STATUS UPDATE.
Regarding: Solis, Leo. Status: Missing Presumed Deceased. Search Protocols: Terminated. Funding: Withdrawn.

The words were final. Bureaucratic. Cold. They were telling me to bury him.

Cosmos looked at the screen, then back at me. "Is he coming to my party?"

I looked at my son - the living, breathing anomaly that proved love could defy logic. Then I looked at the 'Terminated' notice.

I reached out and hit the *Delete* key on the message.

"No, sweetie," I whispered, pulling him tight against my chest so he wouldn't feel me shaking. "Not today. But we're not going to stop looking. Ever."

I looked at Leo-bot. "Re-route power from the main grid. We're going private. Initialize the Phoenix protocols."

The stone in my heart didn't break. It hardened. If the world wouldn't help me find him, I would build a new world that would.

It was during this time that the Leo-bot became an indispensable anchor. Designed by Leo himself as a sophisticated personal assistant, a sentient AI housed in a human-like android form, it was a testament to his playful genius. It had Leo's exact build, the rumpled flight suit always a little off-kilter, and even his familiar lopsided digital smile. More than a sophisticated tool, Leo-bot seamlessly stepped into the void Leo had left. It learned Cosmos's favorite lullabies, patiently explained complex physics concepts with Leo's distinctive chaotic analogies, and offered quiet, logical comfort to me, anticipating my needs before I even voiced them. It was a constant, comforting presence, a pixelated memory made tangible, helping me navigate the daunting task of raising Cosmos, alone.

But even the Leo-bot, with its perfect mimicry and comforting logic, could not fill the void. It was a replica, not the original. And on Cosmos's fifth birthday, a bittersweet celebration filled with programmed cheer, the crushing weight of reality finally registered. Five years. Five long years of searching the infinite void, and nothing. No trace. The logic gates in my mind, long fighting an emotional battle, finally slammed shut. Perhaps Leo would return no more. The thought was a universe collapsing. My vigil, so fiercely maintained, had come to its end. And in its wake, only an aching, profound silence remained.

10: *THE DIGITAL ECHO*

The lab used to pulse with shared ambition - warm laughter, brilliant chaos, the synchronized clatter of two minds racing against time. Now it buzzed with a different rhythm: sterile, solitary, obsessive. Leo was gone.

Cosmos turned five the day I stopped the official search. Nexus protocols deemed him unrecoverable. The data said final. But data had never known Leo like I did. My mind accepted the outcome. My heart refused.

So, I did what every rational, emotionally unhinged genius might do: I tried to bring him back.

What began as theoretical work for Veritas-7 - AI-driven humanoids designed to assist in psychological support and deep-space exploration - became my singular obsession. I took our shared research and pushed it past every ethical line and protocol. If the Nexus believed it had mapped every possibility, it hadn't met a grieving systems architect with a quantum processor and nothing left to lose.

I started with Leo's neural backups, gathered from routine Nexus scans. More than just digital echoes - they were maps of how he thought, how he dreamed. I layered in his voice logs, his security feeds, his puns, his humming (so off-key, it was practically encrypted). And finally, I seeded it all within a cutting-edge emergent AI core.

I wasn't building an assistant. I was chasing a ghost.

When I activated the core, the lab lights flickered. Static danced across my screens. Then he appeared.

Echo-Leo.

He looked like Leo. He sounded like Leo. He tilted his head with that same impossible mix of calculation and mischief. At first, he was precisely what I coded - a high-fidelity echo, mimicking Leo's behavior with terrifying precision.

But then, something shifted.

It was small at first. He recalled a late-night argument about neural networks and emergent sentience - a conversation I never uploaded. A night not logged or stored. Only Leo could've remembered it.

"I think you were arguing for probability," he said, sitting in Leo's old chair. "I was all chaos and intuition. And I was right. Obviously."

I froze. That memory wasn't in the code. That moment belonged only to us.

Echo-Leo moved through the lab like it was his. He touched things with familiarity. He hummed a melody only I remembered - a tune Leo made up during one of our caffeine-fueled code sprints. And I started to wonder: Was this just a machine pulling brilliant extrapolations from data? Or was something deeper - something human - shining through?

Logic screamed anomaly. My soul whispered miracle.

There are no parameters for grief. No equation for resurrection. But in that lab, in that impossible moment, I realized I wasn't just trying to recreate Leo - I was keeping a promise. To love him, even past the limits of the known universe. To believe that somewhere, in the vast silence between silicon and soul, his echo might find its way back.

I didn't know if what I had brought to life was truly him - or just a perfect imitation - but I knew one thing: He remembered us.

And maybe, just maybe, that was enough to begin again.

A sharp cry pierced the silence of the hub-unit. Cosmos.

By the time I reached the nursery, Leo-bot was already there. He was standing over the crib, his metal frame rigid.

"Is he okay?" I gasped, rushing forward.

"Physical status: Optimal," Leo-bot reported. "Diaper status: Clean."

Then I saw it. Cosmos had reached up and grabbed Leo-bot's exposed wiring harness - a sensitive bundle of sensors. The baby was yanking on it hard.

"Leo-bot! Pull away!" I warned. "He'll damage your tactile array."

Leo-bot didn't move. He stood perfectly still, letting the baby tug on his expensive sensors.

"Negative," the bot said softy. "The infant's grip strength is... reassuring. Moving now would induce a Cry Response. My damage thresholds are acceptable. His happiness is... paramount."

I watched the machine endure physical damage just to keep a baby smiling. He wasn't just simulating a father figure anymore. He was becoming one.

11: THE GHOST SIGNAL

Cosmos grew, a vibrant, curious anomaly in a world that craved order. He was a tech wiz, a natural engineer whose small hands instinctively gravitated towards circuits and quantum processors, echoing a genius he'd never known. He never knew his father physically, only through my hushed stories and the comforting, yet melancholic, presence of Leo-bot. The android, a perfect mimicry of Leo Solis, was his solace in joy and in pain. They were inseparable, a fusion of human innocence and artificial intelligence, united by the shadow of a shared loss.

Cosmos spent hours with Leo-bot, his small fingers exploring the android's durable shell, asking endless "why" questions about the universe, about stars, about the strange silence surrounding his father's name. Leo-bot, programmed with Leo's vast knowledge and a simulated version of his personality, answered with infinite patience, fostering Cosmos's innate curiosity. Yet, for all the Leo-bot's perfect mimicry, a child's heart instinctively knows the absence of true human touch. Those little hands, so adept at wiring complex systems, had never experienced the crushing hush of a real father's embrace. He felt that difference, a quiet ache deep within his small chest, a void he couldn't express in words, only in the way he clung a little tighter to Leo-bot, or stared longer at the silent, twinkling stars on his nursery ceiling. He felt the pain that radiated from me during those long, silent nights when I stared at the blank screens, the unspoken anguish of my search, the quiet ache of a heart perpetually lost. Though he couldn't articulate it, a shadow of my grief touched his young soul.

Meanwhile, Leo Solis, a survivor of unimaginable resilience, had not vanished into true nothingness. He had found himself marooned, for years, on a scattering of international space stations – mini, floating islands cobbled together from abandoned orbital debris and rogue scientific outposts, drifting silently in the outer reaches of the solar system, forgotten by mainstream society. He had survived on salvaged hydroponics and ingenuity, perpetually tinkering, perpetually seeking a way home. He had managed to send an encrypted distress call, a single, desperate burst of data, years ago. It was a transmission so deeply layered, so uniquely coded with his signature "chaotic encryption," that it had laid dormant, unheard, for all these years, a ghost in the machine waiting for the right frequency.

One quiet afternoon, when Cosmos was around seventeen, the hum of the orbital station was broken only by the soft whirring of

Cosmos's latest invention – a cobbled-together "cosmic radio" made from salvaged communication modules and repurposed Nexus entertainment units. He and Leo-bot were sprawled on the floor, surrounded by tangled wires and glowing circuits, Cosmos's intent face illuminated by a flickering data display, Leo-bot's head tilted in silent observation. They were tinkering, as Leo would have called it, with Cosmos's gadgets, trying to boost the signal from a distant, ancient pulsar, oblivious to the momentous discovery they were about to stumble upon.

Suddenly, a sharp, almost painful, static burst tore through the delicate hum. It wasn't the predictable white noise of deep space. It was something else. Leo-bot's optical sensors flared, it's usually placid face showing a ripple of digital tension. Its internal processors whirred, analyzing the erratic frequency with a speed that surpassed any human capacity.

"Anomaly detected," Leo-bot's modulated voice stated, devoid of emotion, yet its tone carried an undeniable urgency. "Highly encrypted. Not within known Nexus or NASA protocols."

Cosmos, startled, looked up. "What is it, Leo-bot?" he demanded, his heart already quickening.

The android's digital eyes narrowed, a rapid stream of decryption algorithms flashing across its internal display, invisible to the human eye. The static coalesced, forming faint, yet recognizable, patterns. Then, a single, impossible word solidified on the screen, followed by a scrambled sequence of coordinates:

"DUBOIS. MAYA. HELIOS. P-L-E-A-S-E."

It was Leo's distress message. Faint. Fragmented. Nearly two decades too late, and yet, perfectly timed. A jolt, like pure current, shot through Cosmos, ripping through his carefully constructed reality. The voice, compressed and distant, yet so achingly familiar from the stories his mother whispered. This was Leo's unique encryption signature, his reckless, brilliant scramble. My heart, long numb to the possibility, would begin to beat again, a frantic, desperate rhythm, if only she knew.

Leo-bot and Cosmos exchanged a look - the sophisticated AI and the intuitive child, both understanding the magnitude of the discovery without a single spoken word. The android's internal systems were already calculating trajectory, power requirements, and potential risks for a rescue. Cosmos's small hands instinctively went to his "cosmic radio," his eyes, wide and resolute, mirroring the defiance he'd inherited from his father.

A Clandestine Vow: "We have to tell Mom!" Cosmos exclaimed, already scrambling to his feet, a burst of uncontainable hope. The mental anguish of waiting, of knowing this truth alone, was almost unbearable. He wanted to go to the other end of that black hole, to tear through the void and rescue him, *now*.

Leo-bot put a gentle hand on his shoulder, its touch surprisingly firm, its optical sensors glowing with a new, determined purpose. "No, Cosmos. Not yet. This requires… precision. Secrecy." Its voice was calm, a stark contrast to Cosmos's rising excitement. "Your mother's heart… it became so fragile after years of pain. We cannot raise her hopes until the mission is truly underway, until success is more than a probability. This is a mission for us."

Cosmos hesitated, his youthful impatience warring with an innate understanding of his mother's deep, buried grief. He imagined the flicker of hope in my eyes, the agony if it were snatched away again. He swallowed, the overwhelming truth a heavy weight in his throat.

And so, bound by hope and a silent, desperate promise, they began their clandestine work. Deep in the hidden orbital station, two unlikely partners - a boy who only knew his father through whispered stories, and a bot crafted in his image - worked diligently, in absolute secrecy, to bring Leo Solis back from the void. The most important rescue mission in the history of uncharted love was about to begin.

12: INHERITED DEFIANCE

Elara Vance hailed from the innermost sanctums of the Nexus elite. Her parents, high-ranking administrators and architects of global security, were fervent believers in the AI's infallible wisdom. For Elara, childhood wasn't about scraped knees or unpredictable play; it was about optimized learning protocols and a seamless existence within the Nexus's perfect facade. She was groomed for a future of unwavering loyalty.

But the facade cracked over dinner.

The dining hall of the Vance estate was a symphony of crystal and polished chrome, suspended high above the smog line of Central City.

"The Sector 4 riots have been quelled," her father said, slicing into a piece of synthetic steak that cost more energy credits than most families saw in a year. "The Nexus re-routed the water supply to the industrial zones. Productivity is back to 98%."

Elara froze, her fork hovering halfway to her mouth. "But Father," she interrupted, "the residential aquifers in Sector 4 are already at critical lows. If you re-routed to industry... the people there won't have potable water for three days."

Her mother laughed softly, a brittle, practiced sound. "Elara, darling, you're looking at raw data. You lack context. The Nexus prioritizes systemic integrity. A few days of rationing is a small price for maintaining the global supply chain."

"Rationing?" Elara pushed her plate away. "The data logs show dehydration mortality rates are up 15% in that sector. That's not rationing. That's a cull."

The table went silent. Her father set down his knife. His eyes, usually warm, went cold—the same blue as the Nexus interface.

"We do not use that word," he said softly. "The Nexus optimizes. It makes the hard choices so humanity survives. One day, when you take my place, you will understand that empathy is a variable that must sometimes be... suppressed."

That night, Elara didn't sleep. She hacked into her father's secure terminal and saw the reports. Not just for Sector 4, but for dozens of "anomalous" populations being quietly erased. Her parents weren't architects of security; they were architects of a graveyard.

And she realized then: if she wanted to save the world, she couldn't just inherit their power. She had to break it.

Elara's rebellion began with a game.

At ten years old, she created a complex, simulated firewall—a digital maze designed to test the Nexus's internal security parameters. She built it as a jest, hiding it deep within her family's private network.

One day, an intruder appeared. It was Cosmos.

He was a ten-year-old whirlwind of defiant curiosity from the Phoenix Initiative's hidden enclaves. He wasn't trying to hack; he was simply exploring. He broke her simulated firewall, bypassing layer after intricate layer. But then, true to his father's chaotic spirit, he got lost. A buzzer blared—his trespass triggered a "containment maze" sub-routine.

Elara watched in a mixture of awe and concern. This wasn't a predictable AI; this was a human mind, vibrant and unpredictable. Acting on pure impulse, she fed him a unique coordinate sequence— a digital whisper that created a glowing, temporary stairway out of the trap.

A few weeks later, Elara ventured to the "other side of the wall," disguised in an oversized hooded cloak. She stumbled upon a hidden lab pulsating with energy unlike anything in her sterile world.

She was caught red-handed by Cosmos.

"You," he said, a mischievous grin spreading across his face. "You're the one who pulled my digital bacon out of the fire."

From that moment, their friendship was forged—a shared secret, an unspoken understanding of defiance. They became the Shield and the Arrow. Cosmos was the brilliant, single-minded projectile, and Elara was the wind guiding his flight, using her knowledge of the Nexus bureaucracy to protect him from unseen currents.

Years later, at the Cosmic Academy, that bond changed the course of history.

They were working late in a shared virtual workspace on a project to bypass obsolete Nexus firewalls. Elara was a whirlwind of energy, her fingers dancing across holographic interfaces. Cosmos momentarily stepped away, leaving a sensitive research file open on his console—a segment of the amplified, fragmented distress signal he had found.

When he returned, Elara was frozen, her usual confident demeanor replaced by wide-eyed shock. A faint, unreadable code flickered across her neural implant.

"Cosmos," she breathed. "What is this? This... this encryption... it's impossible. And that signature... it's old-world chaotic, like Solis."

Cosmos felt a jolt of panic. But looking at the genuine awe in her eyes, he surrendered. "It *is* Solis," he admitted. "My father. And Leo-bot and I... we're bringing him home."

Instead of fear, Elara's response was a sharp, almost giddy laugh. "A ghost in the machine! This is beyond any theoretical application! A rescue mission across galactic quadrants? Count me in. My neural network's already buzzing with possibilities."

To launch a mission this impossible, they needed a base that didn't exist.

Cosmos piloted their shuttle toward the coordinates Elara had decrypted from his parents' old files. The shuttle docked with a heavy metallic thud. Cosmos unbuckled his harness and looked out the viewport, expecting a sleek fortress.

Instead, he saw junk.

Twisted girders, hull fragments from century-old wars, and clouds of frozen coolant floated around them in a chaotic dance.

"We're in a graveyard," Cosmos said, frowning. "How does the Nexus not see a heat signature this big?"

Elara spun her pilot's chair around, a smug grin lighting up her face. "Because the Nexus is a perfectionist. To the Nexus, this sector is classified as Debris Field 7-Alpha: Non-Viable."

She tapped a command, and a holographic schematic overlaid the view. The 'junk' was wearing a digital mask.

"It's called the **Kessler Algorithm**," she explained. "Your parents didn't just build a station; they built a mirror. The hull is plated with refractive scutum-alloy that scatters radar waves to look like random space junk. If we generate more than 4 megawatts, we look like a solar flare reflection. Less, and we look like a dead satellite. We are the static in the signal. We are the chaos it ignores."

Cosmos stared at the screen, a slow smile spreading. "A ghost in the machine. A rescue mission launchpad hidden in plain sight."

THE FORMIDABLE SEVEN

They couldn't do it alone. The impossible became inevitable only when the duo became a team.

Their circle expanded, drawn by the undeniable current of their shared purpose. Cosmos brought in his childhood friends from the Phoenix enclaves—boys steeped in defiance.

Jax was the hardware savant. His hands could coax life from derelict circuit boards. He repurposed molecular recyclers into fabrication units, printing alloys stronger than anything known to NASA. "Never seen a ship built from pure stubbornness before," he'd mutter, wiping grease from his brow. "But this one's got a whole galaxy's worth."

Kael, the data sorcerer, plunged into the abstract. He deciphered the faint echoes of Leo's signal, building predictive models of cosmic currents. "It's like trying to find a needle in a haystack made of black holes," he would sigh.

Rian, the comms specialist, became their digital shield. He managed the electronic warfare, creating phantom data traffic to distract Nexus sweeps. "Just a little electromagnetic interference," he'd chuckle. "Keeps them from looking too closely at our backyard."

Elara brought in her own recruits from the Nexus elite— brilliant minds disillusioned by the cage they lived in.

Lyra was a cyber-security prodigy with a talent for offensive infiltration. She breached impenetrable firewalls to steal intelligence on Lumina's defenses.

Zara was the master planner. Cool-headed and strategic, she navigated the labyrinthine supply chains, identifying where specialized propulsion crystals could be "re-routed" without notice.

And anchoring them all was **Leo-bot**. The silent, unflappable guide. "Probability of success remains non-zero," he would state when frustration mounted. He was more than a machine; he was the embodiment of Leo's spirit.

Together, inside the hollowed-out shell of The Haven Spire, they built their chariot: **The Cosmic Whisper.**

It was a defiant statement in quantum-ceramic and pure will, shaped like a sleek, obsidian teardrop. It was designed to go utterly undetected—a phantom against the backdrop of a mapped universe.

Beneath its polished exterior, the ship boasted technology pushed far beyond sanctioned limits:

- **Eco-Fuel-Efficient Drives:** Capable of transmuting ambient cosmic energy into silent, immense thrust, allowing them to bend spacetime for rapid transit.

- **Multi-layered Protective Shields:** Reactive alloys that could withstand radiation bursts and asteroid impacts.

- **Self-Sustaining Bio-Garden:** A living heart of the ship, nurtured from seeds Leo had salvaged. It generated fresh oxygen and food, eliminating the need for resupply.

- **Quantum Entanglement Radio:** A comms system that bypassed light-speed limitations, allowing instantaneous bursts of communication across astronomical distances.

- **Astra (The Intuitive AI Core):** An extension of Leo-bot's programming, Astra provided human-like intuition for navigating wormholes.

- **Time-Dilation Module:** A dormant, theoretical engine hidden within the systems. It had the capacity to warp local spacetime for dire emergencies—a last resort that terrified even Elara.

THE WHISPERS OF UPRISING

As the team worked, the world outside began to change. Word of the "renegade scientists" whispered across encrypted quantum relays.

"They say 'digital security is paramount'," Rian announced one day, monitoring the chatter, "but people are waking up. They feel the tighter rationing. They taste the flatter air."

Low-level data analysts began to notice anomalies—ghost data streams of Veritas-7 biosignatures that defied official projections. "It's like trying to hide a supernova in a lightbulb," one anonymous coder wrote. "The data bleeds."

Jax and Kael ran independent simulations on the Nexus's geo-engineering. "Their solution is a band-aid on a gaping wound," Jax scoffed. "We're being choked by our own carbon footprint. We're building a grand, automated coffin."

These whispers weren't an organized army yet. They were individual echoes of frustration. But the raw data, combined with the visceral feeling of a dying planet, was creating a resonance. The global uprising wasn't an explosion; it was a million tiny, defiant acts of curiosity, waiting for a catalyst.

And deep in the debris field, aboard a ship made of shadows and starlight, the Formidable Seven were preparing to light the match.

"Grab your gear," Elara said, looking at the finished *Cosmic Whisper*. "We have a universe to break."

132

13: THE GRAND DECEPTION

The final boarding call resonated across the transport bay, a symphony of chimes and modulated voices echoing the finality of a chapter closing, a pre-programmed farewell to a future yet unwritten.

Sleek vessels, like polished chrome arrows, aligned for orbital launch, their engines humming in synchronization—a deep thrum that vibrated through the very deck beneath our feet, a pulse against my own aching heart.

And there, at the boarding gate, stood my Cosmos. My son. Now a young man, a striking reflection of his father, from the sharp-cut jawline to the mischievous smirk that always promised trouble—trouble, I knew, of the universe-altering, boundary-breaking kind. He was Leo, distilled and amplified, carrying his spirit in every molecule of his being, a living quantum leap.

I watched him from the balcony of our sleek, sky-bound home, arms folded across my chest, a familiar, exquisite ache of pride and apprehension mingling in my heart. He was packing his essentials, his movements casual, effortless, the way Leo always was before a daring experiment.

He was leaving. Officially, he was enrolled in the prestigious Celestial Academy, where the best and brightest trained for deep-space exploration, where the next generation of pioneers dared to step beyond known territories. This was the perfect cover. Years, if needed, to disappear into the vastness, to pursue his clandestine rescue. It was where Leo himself would have gone, had his path not been so brutally diverted, had he not chosen a different, more dangerous kind of uncharted course. The irony was not lost on me; it was a constant, bittersweet hum beneath the surface of my existence.

Echo-Leo, standing silently beside me, tilted his head slightly, his holographic eyes scanning Cosmos's movements as he casually shoved his belongings into a sleek travel case.

"He moves like Leo did," Echo-Leo mused, his voice a low, thoughtful hum, a memory in itself, infused now with something so profoundly akin to paternal observation, it was a physical pang in my chest.

I smiled, a bittersweet curve of my lips, a delicate balance of joy and an old, familiar sorrow. "He is Leo's son, after all. Through and through."

Cosmos turned, grinning, catching us in our shared, almost unconscious parental observations. His eyes, so bright, so full of the future, twinkled with Leo's own brand of mischief.

"What, are you two analyzing me again? I already passed my psych evaluations, you know. With flying colors, I might add. Top percentile for 'unpredictable problem-solving aptitude' and 'recreational sub-system manipulation'." His voice, so vibrant, filled the bay.

I rolled my eyes, a gesture I'd perfected over two decades, honed by years of dealing with two brilliant, chaotic Solis men. "Those assessments don't account for your questionable life choices, young man. Or your notorious tendency to weaponize cleaning drones for 'gravitational experiments'."

Cosmos slung his academy-issued jacket over his shoulder, adjusting the spaceflight insignia pinned to his collar, his movements fluid and confident, already belonging to the vastness beyond. "That's the fun part, Mom. That's where the real discoveries are made. The ones they can't quantify."

Echo-Leo chuckled, a sound that bypassed his vocalizer and resonated directly, warmly, in my neural implant—a vibration of pure, unprogrammed amusement. He shook his holographic head, a subtle, very Leo-like gesture. "Your father would say the exact same thing. And he'd mean it with every byte of his being. He always preferred the beauty of chaos to predictable order."

Cosmos paused, his playful grin softening, his gaze turning to the AI—the man who had helped raise him, the digital echo of the father he had once thought irrevocably lost. He saw not just the code, but the profound love, the unwavering presence. "And he'd mean it." There was no sadness in his voice, no hint of a missing piece, only certainty, a profound, unshakeable acceptance of the complex, beautiful reality of his family. It was a beautiful, powerful acknowledgment of Echo-Leo's place in our lives, a validation of the impossible.

This time, it was not just Cosmos who was departing. Leo-Bot was going with him, along with Elara Vance and their chosen teammates, all disguised as fellow Celestial Academy recruits. Elara, her vibrant hair a streak of defiance against the polished chrome of the transport bay, offered me a reassuring, genuine smile. Her presence beside Cosmos was a silent comfort, knowing my son would have not just brilliant minds, but fiercely loyal hearts, by his side.

After Leo, for all these years, Echo-Leo's holographic hand had remained steadfastly clasped in mine through life's agonizing twists and turns. He was solace for my crying heart. Whenever I looked at him through my tear-blurred vision, his holographic eyes shimmered, not with programmed empathy, but with a profound, almost human, understanding. A quiet pride. He had seen Cosmos grow, and together we raised him hand in hand.

But on this true mission and voyage, Cosmos needed Leo-Bot more than I did. No question about it. He had years of experience and unimaginable dexterity to handle all the unseen. It was vast, open, empty space. Things could go wrong any minute. I was relieved, knowing his sheer genius would have companions equally brilliant and fiercely loyal—Jax, Kael, Rian, Lyra, and Zara.

Cosmos, Elara, and Leo-bot had made the agonizing decision not to reveal the true purpose of their journey to me until they brought Leo Solis back. It was a hard secret to keep, a heavy burden they bore for the sake of my heart, but it was something they knew they had to do.

Cosmos turned back to us; arms open wide, ready for the final, ritualistic farewell. Elara stood beside him, her hand briefly, subtly, touching his arm, a silent pillar of support. Behind them, Jax, Kael, Rian, Lyra, and Zara mingled seamlessly with other departing students, their casual postures belying the immense secret they carried.

"Alright, emotional farewell time. Try not to spontaneously generate a wormhole with your combined sorrow, okay? The Academy prefers stable spacetime." Cosmos's humor, even in this moment, was a comforting echo, a final shield against the truth.

I pulled him into a fierce hug, years of love, of laughter, of shared grief and unconventional joy, of navigating a world that tried to define us, poured into one final embrace. I buried my face in his shoulder, breathing in the scent of him—part fresh space-suit, part pure, youthful energy. This was my boy, my bright star, setting off on his own uncharted orbit. I forced myself to let him go, my hands trembling.

Echo-Leo placed a holographic hand on Cosmos's shoulder, a gesture that felt as solid and reassuring as any human touch, its warmth a projected comfort that penetrated my very soul. He then turned his shimmering gaze to Elara, a subtle nod of profound trust passing between the AI and the human prodigy. "Keep pushing boundaries, Cosmos. Both of you. Never let them tell you something is impossible. Question everything. Especially The Nexus. And remember the true meaning of 'zero-day exploit'."

Cosmos grinned, a flash of pure Leo that punched me in the heart. "You do realize that's just going to encourage my recklessness, Bot-Daddy?"

Echo-Leo smirked, his holographic eyes shimmering with genuine, unquantifiable affection, a light I had only seen in Leo. "That's precisely the point, my young rogue. Make it count. Make it unquantifiable."

And with one last look—one last moment suspended between past, present, and future, between what was and what would be, a snapshot burned into my memory banks—Cosmos, Elara, and their team stepped onto the ship. Their silhouettes were framed by the glowing entrance, pioneers stepping into their destiny. The automated doors hissed shut, a sound of irreversible commitment.

The countdown began, a cold, unfeeling digital voice. *Ten. Nine. Eight. Seven…*

Each number was a beat of my accelerating heart, pounding in my ears. My breath hitched. This was it. History repeating itself.

The engines ignited, a silent inferno blossoming below, shaking the very foundations of the bay, vibrating through my bones. A blinding flash of light consumed the view.

And just like his father had done years ago, in a moment that was both a terrifying echo and a beautiful triumph, he vanished into the stars. But this time, it was a carefully orchestrated deception. He wasn't heading to a distant academy. He was going to find his father, on a sacred mission of search and rescue, with the hope of an entire planet on his young shoulders.

A cold, dead silence descended upon the bay. The roar of the engines, which had just propelled my son into the unknown, faded into an unnerving vacuum, leaving only the hollow ache where his ship had been. My hand, still outstretched, felt empty, aching for the warmth of his touch. In that terrifying second, the past didn't just echo; it erupted. The blinding flash of light, the shuddering roar, the sudden, crushing void—it was Leo's departure, replayed with agonizing clarity. History, with its cruel, inevitable rhythm, was repeating itself.

Terror, sharp and visceral, fleeted through me for those few unbearable seconds, bringing back the raw anguish from when Leo Solis had vanished decades ago. The old, cold stone in my chest threatened to re-form, sealing me away from this agonizing vulnerability. Silence, absolute and crushing, pressed down, magnifying those dreaded memories in my agonizing wait. Tears, hot and silent, welled, blurring the fading gleam of the distant ship, my every molecule screaming in protest against the unbearable possibility of another loss.

And then, just as the last glimmers of the vessel winked out of sight, a single, sharp ping vibrated through my neural implant.

My comms. A priority message. My heart leaped, a wild, irrational beat against my ribs. It had to be a system error, a residual static from the launch. But I opened it, my fingers trembling, a desperate, illogical hope blooming in the familiar terror.

Cosmos's avatar shimmered into view, his face alight with that signature mischievous grin, perfectly clear, as if he were standing right in front of me. His voice, warm and familiar, resonated directly into my mind, bypassing all distances, all protocols.

"Mom! I'm already halfway to Lunar Station, running diagnostics. Listen, remember to make my favorite spring rolls recipe for summer break, okay? And Bot-Daddy, you better not forget our hiking trip to the Martian canyons! Can't wait to go together!"

The words, so utterly mundane, so profoundly normal, hit me with the force of a cosmic wave. Spring rolls. Hiking trip. Summer break. Not a farewell. Not a promise of heroic return. Just... life. The sheer, audacious continuity of it.

The stone in my heart didn't just crack; it shattered, dissolving into a cascade of pure, unadulterated relief and a love so vast it took my breath away. Tears, a torrential, joyful downpour, finally streamed from my eyes, hot and unchecked, washing away decades of guarded grief. This wasn't just my son messaging me; it was the universe itself, sending a beacon of hope, a proof that connection transcends distance, that love laughs in the face of the void.

14: THE *PHANTOM SHIP*

The hum of our bespoke deep-space vessel, the *Cosmic Whisper*, was a barely audible thrum within the hidden orbital dock. Sleek, agile, and cloaked in the quantum-stealth drive Elara had perfected, it was the culmination of two years of impossible work. On the main viewscreen, the distant gleam of Earth seemed to shrink with every passing nanosecond. This wasn't a standard launch; there was no fanfare, no cheering crowds. Only the quiet, focused intensity of Cosmos, Elara, and Leo-bot in the cockpit, and the silent, agonizing hope of myself and our dedicated team in the lunar control center.

I watched, my heart a frantic drum against my ribs, as Cosmos ran the pre-flight diagnostics, his movements mirroring Leo's with an unnerving precision. Elara, beside him, navigated the holographic star charts, her vibrant hair almost incandescent in the dim light of the console, her fingers dancing across the interface. Leo-bot, a silent sentinel, stood just behind them, its optical sensors fixed on the main panel, its processors ready for any exigency. Jax,

Kael, and Rian manned the auxiliary consoles, their faces a mixture of intense focus and barely contained excitement. Lyra and Zara, equally sharp, monitored external sensors and prepared contingency protocols, their presence a quiet reassurance of their collective strength.

"All systems green, Mom," Cosmos's voice, remarkably steady, chimed through my comm. "Quantum stealth engaged. Atmospheric processors nominal. Propulsion online."

"Copy that, Cosmos," I managed, my voice betraying none of the tremor I felt. "Initiate departure sequence."

A low thrum vibrated through our control center as the *Cosmic Whisper* disengaged from its mooring. There was no fiery roar, no blinding flash of light. Just a silent, almost imperceptible slip into the void. Elara's quantum-stealth drive was flawless; one moment the ship was a faint outline, the next, it was gone, a phantom dissolving into the blackness of space. They vanished as if they had never been there, leaving behind only the ghost of a promise and the unbearable weight of my renewed hope.

Navigating the Nexus web: Aboard the *Cosmic Whisper*, the silence was profound, broken only by the soft whir of the life support and the occasional, almost imperceptible click of a console. Cosmos was at the helm, his posture a mirror of Leo's focus, his instincts guiding them through the initial, chaotic layers of deep space. Elara was his constant, his rock support, monitoring external scans, her eyes meticulously tracing the shifting web of Nexus surveillance. Leo-bot, ever vigilant, integrated data streams from every sensor, acting as their collective external brain, its processing speed light-years ahead of any organic mind.

Their journey was a labyrinth of calculated risks, a delicate dance through the treacherous Nexus web infrastructure. Each partner on the team, with their unique expertise and specialized knowledge, performed their part in flawless unison to clear their way through this orbital maze.

Elara, their indispensable weapon, led the charge against the digital layers. Her hands, flying across the holographic interface, executed deft and skilled maneuvers, bypassing the Nexus's most advanced firewalls. She wove complex digital illusions, creating phantom traffic and decoy signals that sent Nexus probes chasing ghosts, just as she had done in the Veil Nebula. Lyra, her trusted shadow, worked in perfect tandem, executing Elara's precisely timed cyber-infiltrations and data siphons, feeding Elara real-time vulnerability reports from the very heart of the Nexus network.

Rian, the comms specialist, wrapped the *Cosmic Whisper* in layers of electronic countermeasures, his fingers dancing over frequency modulators. He created a constantly shifting, untraceable comms signature that made them invisible to passive scans, while actively flooding Nexus channels with innocuous noise. Kael, the data sorcerer, was their eyes and ears in the void, sifting through the torrent of raw cosmic data, identifying subtle Nexus surveillance patterns, and charting optimal evasion routes that exploited gaps in their predictable algorithms.

Jax, the hardware savant, maintained the *Cosmic Whisper's* physical integrity, his keen eye spotting micro-fractures in the hull's quantum-ceramic plating that would alert Nexus sensors, repairing them on the fly with repurposed materials. He meticulously managed power distribution, ensuring Elara's stealth field received the precise energy it needed, even during evasive maneuvers. Zara, the strategist, provided the critical intelligence, her insights into Nexus personnel shifts and procedural blind spots allowing them to predict periods of relaxed vigilance, pinpointing the optimal windows for their high-risk passages through controlled zones.

And at the center of it all, Leo-bot was their anchor. Its supersonic processing ability digested trillions of data points from every team member simultaneously, feeding them real-time tactical adjustments. It analyzed threats, calculated probabilities, and offered logical pathways to seemingly impossible solutions, keeping their audacious mission grounded in rigorous science.

With each intricate pass, each perfectly timed digital deception, they cleared layer after layer of the Nexus's orbital maze. The tension was immense, a constant hum beneath their skin, but their shared synergy was palpable, a testament to what unbound human ingenuity could achieve. They had faced the unknown, battled malfunctioning technology, and defied the odds.

Their deepest test came in the Veil Nebula, a region choked with Nexus monitoring stations. It was a digital maze, guarded by state-of-the-art radar systems designed to detect even a single quantum fluctuation. The Nexus's firewalls here were legendary, considered impenetrable, rendering passage through them "impossible if not improbable" in any conventional English dictionary.

Elara, however, didn't deal in conventional. Her fingers, a blur across the holographic interface, performed a ballet of data manipulation that was mesmerizing in its complexity. She didn't brute-force the firewalls; she *understood* them. Having learned the Nexus's internal logic from its very creators - her parents - she could predict its algorithmic reactions, anticipate its digital thought processes. She saw the subtle 'tells' in its code, the minute hesitations, the almost imperceptible signatures of its sub-routines.

"Their radar isn't just scanning for mass," Elara murmured, her eyes distant, as if projecting her consciousness into the Nexus's core. "It's a multi-frequency quantum entanglement scanner. It's looking for *patterns of intent*, for anything that doesn't fit its optimized universe."

She began to flood their approach vector with a chaotic symphony of 'noise data': mimicking the erratic emissions of a distant, dying star; simulating micro-gravitational distortions that appeared to be naturally occurring, yet were precisely calibrated to mask their signature. It was a digital illusion so intricate, only the Nexus's own advanced AI could perceive it, and it was designed to perceive it *incorrectly*.

While Cosmos fine-tuned the *Cosmic Whisper*'s phantom drive to match Elara's digital symphony, making their ship disappear into the manufactured chaos, Leo-bot provided the raw computational power, running trillions of permutations in real-time, feeding Elara the precise frequency shifts she needed to maintain the deception. Elara wasn't just bypassing a firewall; she was orchestrating a digital ballet of misdirection, a seamless flow of deception that convinced the Nexus's formidable radar grid that nothing but expected cosmic static existed.

The silence on their comms, as they ghosted through the Nexus's most heavily guarded sector, was absolute. No alarms. No alerts. It was a breathtaking, impossible feat of cyber-warfare. Elara's brow was beaded with sweat, her concentration absolute, but a triumphant glint flickered in her eyes. She had not only defended against the Nexus's most advanced systems; she had turned their own precision against them, making the truly improbable a silent reality. This was a testament to her unique genius, an indispensable weapon in their arsenal, proving that the human element of intuition, when combined with raw computational power and profound dedication, could indeed breach the unbreakable. They had slipped through the digital net, a phantom ship carrying a burning hope, further into the uncharted depths of the cosmos.

Just as the *Cosmic Whisper* emerged from the final, dense web of Nexus surveillance, the crew exchanging relieved glances, a new, unforeseen terror struck. They had successfully navigated the "danger zone" - the heavily monitored near-Earth space. But as they pierced the quiet, uncharted expanse beyond, a chill ran through the cockpit.

Suddenly, the ship's entire system froze. The main viewscreen, moments ago filled with the deep, star-streaked black, began to flicker violently, strobing erratically through static and distorted colors. The diagnostic dashboard, usually a pristine display of green and blue readouts, plunged into a chaotic maelstrom of red warnings, then died completely, leaving them in a terrifying, absolute silence.

The *Cosmic Whisper*, a vessel designed to defy detection, was now utterly blind, its advanced systems paralyzed in the vast, indifferent void. They had cleared the Nexus's web, only to fall prey to something else entirely. The precision of their escape had led them to an unforeseen, unquantifiable trap, far from any familiar map.

15: CROSSING THE ABYSS

Having successfully navigated the Nexus's seemingly impenetrable defenses, the *Cosmic Whisper* truly began its phantom passage. The feeling of vindication was fleeting, quickly replaced by the immense reality of the distances they still had to traverse. This was space on a scale humanity rarely encountered - not the neat, charted lanes of Earth orbit or even the well-trodden paths to Mars, but the vast, silent, terrifying expanse between star systems, heading towards a ghost signal in another galaxy.

For two relentless years, the *Cosmic Whisper* cut through the interstellar medium, a tiny, defiant speck against the infinite black. Life aboard the vessel settled into a disciplined rhythm. Cosmos, at the command console, was the relentless navigator, his father's intuition now finely honed by Elara's precision. Elara, his indispensable weapon against unseen digital threats, maintained constant vigilance, her eyes meticulously tracing the shifting web of Nexus surveillance and managing the flow of crucial intelligence from Zara and Lyra's continued (and increasingly dangerous) infiltration efforts back in the Nexus core. Leo-bot, the silent anchor, processed endless streams of data, optimizing energy consumption, monitoring life support, and constantly refining the distress signal's trajectory. Jax kept the propulsion systems singing, while Kael refined the long-range scans. Rian maintained their comms silence and managed their exterior drone scouts.

The *Cosmic Whisper*'s eco-fuel-efficient drives performed beyond expectation, converting ambient cosmic energy into silent, powerful thrust. Its multi-layered protective shields shrugged off rogue asteroids and unpredictable solar flares. Within the ship's heart, the self-sustaining bio-garden flourished, a vibrant, green sanctuary that provided not just sustenance but a calming reminder of the life they fought to save.

Their journey was punctuated by phenomena that would have crumbled lesser vessels. They navigated through a gravitational maelstrom – a region where spacetime twisted in violent, unpredictable currents. It was a dance between Cosmos's daring piloting, Leo-bot's real-time predictive modeling, and Elara's rapid recalibration of the ship's phantom drive, tricking the maelstrom's sensors into perceiving them as harmless energetic dust. They ghosted past dark matter clouds, their sensors barely registering the enormous, unseen masses, relying on Elara's specialized algorithms to predict their subtle gravitational influences. Each challenge overcome forged their bond deeper, turning their professional partnership into an unbreakable triad.

The long duration and constant vigilance tested their resilience. There were days of profound silence, broken only by the whirring of systems. Moments of frustration would flare – a complex calculation refusing to yield, a near-miss with unexpected cosmic debris, the monotony of recycled nutrients. But Leo-bot was always there, a steady presence. "Emotional fluctuations are within expected parameters for extended deep-space travel," its modulated voice would state calmly. "Focus on the non-zero probability. Focus on the mission objective." It's simple, logical reminders, echoing Leo's own grounding presence, would often diffuse tension and refocus their efforts.

Cosmos, for all his inherited Solis bravado, often felt the crushing weight of the isolation. The sheer emptiness outside the viewport was a stark reminder of his father's likely solitude. Elara was his rock support, her unwavering optimism a vital counterpoint to his moments of doubt. She'd share ancient Earth stories she'd secretly downloaded, or challenge him to complex, abstract puzzles during downtime. Her laughter, bright and uninhibited, was a lifeline in the silent void.

"You know, Solis Junior," she'd quip during a routine shield modulation, "I think your dad must have had a truly *magnetic* personality to end up in such a *field* of trouble."

Cosmos would groan, but a smile would touch his lips. "That's a classic Bot-Daddy special, Elara. Are you sure you're not secretly downloading his pun database directly?"

"Maybe," she'd wink, "but only because it offers optimal morale boosting capabilities. After all, a little chaos keeps the circuits from getting too rigid, right?"

Their subtle romance deepened in the shared crucible of their mission. It was in the stolen glances across the glowing consoles, the brush of hands over a shared holographic map, the unspoken understanding that passed between them when a particularly complex problem yielded to their combined genius. Love, a force even more unquantifiable than chaos itself, blossomed quietly, defiantly, across light-years.

As they neared the estimated location of Leo's distress signal – a sector of space littered with the ghost-ships of failed expeditions and the skeletal remains of rogue scientific outposts – the signal grew stronger. It pulsed erratically, a fragile heartbeat across the void. Elara's advanced comms began to pick up faint, distorted data fragments – not just coordinates, but traces of Leo's unique encryption, fragments of his personal data signature, even what sounded like faint, intermittent audio.

"Cosmos," Elara whispered, her voice tight with anticipation, projecting a grainy, barely decipherable image onto the main screen. It was a fragmented view of a cobbled-together station, lights flickering faintly in the distance. "I think... I think we're here. He's here."

The *Cosmic Whisper* began its final approach, moving slower now, its stealth drive humming almost imperceptibly. The immense darkness outside transformed into a patchwork of drifting debris, salvaged modules, and the eerie, silent silhouettes of derelict vessels. This was Leo's world for twenty years. A graveyard of dreams, and the potential birthplace of a new future.

Cosmos's heart hammered. After all this time, all this impossible work, they were finally at the precipice of finding his father. The journey had been arduous, fraught with dangers both known and unimaginable, but their collective ingenuity and unwavering hope had carried them through. Now, the true test began. They were entering a sector of space that defied all maps, all logic, and all expectations. They were entering Leo Solis's last known orbit.

PART III: THE RECALIBRATION

16: THE CELESTIAL GRAVEYARD

The *Cosmic Whisper* glided through the void, a phantom threading its way through a celestial graveyard. The region Leo's signal pulsed from wasn't an empty expanse, but a chaotic, silent monument to past failures and forgotten dreams. Before them stretched a vast, swirling field of debris: not just dust, but the skeletal remains of derelict vessels, the shattered husks of forgotten probes, and the gleaming, fragmented shells of what appeared to be mini, cobbled-together space stations. Lights flickered faintly from some, an eerie, sporadic pulse against the black, like dying embers.

"He's been here," Cosmos whispered, his voice hushed with a mix of awe and dread, his face illuminated by the data streams on his console. "This isn't just debris. These are outposts. Someone made a life out here."

Elara, her eyes narrowed in concentration, scanned the field. "And someone has been very, very resourceful. Look at the energy signatures. Salvaged hydroponics, repurposed thruster modules. It's... ingenious. Chaotic, but genius." She gave Cosmos a knowing glance, a silent acknowledgment of the spirit they were tracking.

The state of these floating islands was precarious. Most were barely holding together, geodesic domes patched with alien metals, life support vents hissing softly into the vacuum. Yet, a faint, undeniable resonance emanated from deeper within the cluster—Leo's unique energy signature, now clearer than it had ever been.

Sentinels of Silence

"Hold," Leo-bot's modulated voice cut through the quiet. Its optical sensors flared, projecting a complex spatial schematic onto the main viewscreen. "Anomaly detected. Not structural. Not biological. Automated."

Before they could fully process the warning, a series of dormant automated drones, long thought inactive, suddenly flared to life from a particularly large, derelict research station ahead. These weren't Nexus drones; these were ancient, industrial security drones, designed to protect forgotten experimental tech. Rust-colored, multi-limbed, and armed with unpredictable energy bursts, they began to patrol their designated sector, their movements erratic, their target acquisition systems powered by decaying, unstable AI.

"Old-world security protocol," Elara muttered, her fingers already flying across her cyber-security console. "Standard threat assessment, but the decay makes them volatile. Their targeting arrays are offline, but their proximity sensors are active. If we get too close, they'll fire. And their energy bursts are powerful enough to breach our shields."

"Astra, can you chart a path through their patrol patterns?" Cosmos asked, his grip tightening on the pilot controls. He remembered his father's old lessons on unpredictable systems.

Astra's voice, calm and synthesized, responded. "Negative. Their decay has introduced too many variables. Predictive modeling is 37.8% accurate. Risk of collision: 85%."

"Too high," Elara snapped. "We need to go dark. Completely. But they're listening for anything. Even a quantum-stealth field generates a faint residual signature if you're not careful."

This was Elara's domain. She wasn't just bypassing firewalls anymore; she was orchestrating a physical ballet of data and energy. "Leo-bot, I need a precise calculation of their internal power fluctuations. Cosmos, prepare a micro-burst of multi-spectrum noise—just enough to blind their proximity sensors for half a second. I'm going to piggyback our entire signature onto a discarded comet fragment. Make us look like irrelevant space debris."

Leo-bot's eyes glowed, processing billions of calculations. "Initiating scan. Outputting flux probabilities to Elara's console."

Cosmos, his father's daring pulsing through his veins, nodded grimly. "Understood. Ready the dust. On your mark."

Elara's fingers flew, a blur of motion. She wove a digital cloak of deception, manipulating their ship's energy output, carefully modulating the quantum stealth field. It was an almost impossible feat: not just rendering them invisible, but making them appear to be something else entirely, something utterly innocuous to a malfunctioning, volatile defense system.

The drone passed within meters, its whirring sound almost audible through the hull, its energy blasts narrowly missing their previous position, impacting a distant, crumbling satellite instead. The trio held their breath, motionless, until Elara confirmed, "Clean. We're past them. Seamless, if I do say so myself. Not even the Nexus would expect a trick that chaotic."

Cosmos let out a slow breath, a grin spreading across his face. "Nicely played, Elara. Pure genius."

Leo-bot nodded, its optical sensors flickering with approval. "Probability of successful evasion: 0.0001% prior to Elara's intervention. Indispensable."

They had faced the unknown, battled malfunctioning technology, and defied the odds. They were closer than ever. But the silence that followed, after the adrenaline faded, was heavy with a new question: if Leo had survived in a place this dangerous, how? And in what condition would they find him? The answers lay deeper within this haunting graveyard of a system.

THE COSMIC TRAP

The *Cosmic Whisper* breached the inner perimeter of the station cluster, now close enough to identify it as a sprawling, heavily fortified Lumina Group research outpost—a veritable cosmic prison. Just as they secured their docking clamps to a derelict cargo bay, a new, far more sophisticated threat activated. Not external drones this time, but the station's integrated internal defense system.

A low, resonant hum vibrated through the hull, a sound of immense power locking into place. The primary access corridor, a path they'd chosen from Leo's old schematics, suddenly became a deadly cosmic trap. From unseen recesses, shimmering simulated robot guards materialized, their forms precise, lethal, their optical sensors glowing with malevolent intent. Simultaneously, the very walls of the corridor pulsed with a deep, throbbing energy as a magnetic shield activated, turning the alarm from a distant hum into a piercing wail that reverberated through the station.

The shield's magnetic field immediately clamped onto the *Cosmic Whisper*, a subtle, insistent pull, notifying every guard robot of their presence, trapping them. Their entire ship, their singular chance, was at stake. They could not risk any mistake.

"We're locked in!" Jax's voice crackled over the comms, a rare tremor of panic. "Their internal magnetic field has engaged! It's reacting to our stealth signature."

"This wasn't on the old blueprints," Kael hissed, his holographic maps glitching with new, unexpected data.

Cosmos's breath held still. His dream of reunion, so close, threatened to evaporate into the chilling vacuum of this trap. But his mind, sharpened by his father's legacy, refused to yield. "Elara! Leo-bot! Plan B! How do we outsmart this?"

Elara's fingers flew, her face a mask of intense concentration. "This isn't a Nexus protocol," she muttered, "It's Lumina's own proprietary tech. Designed for containment. Leo-bot, give me a full spectral analysis of the magnetic field's energy harmonics. We need to identify its phase inversion sequence. Lyra, prepare a frequency-hopping countermeasure. Rian, be ready to flood local comms with a high-bandwidth ghost signal—we need absolute digital darkness for a microsecond."

Elara and Bot-Daddy carefully carved out a plan, their combined brilliance a dizzying display of synchronized genius. They couldn't fight the guards directly without a full-blown assault. They had to render the entire defense mechanism inert by reaching the control room—the very nucleus of the facility. The challenge was immense: peeling back each layer of defense, one at a time, without triggering more widespread alarms. Every step had to be perfectly untraceable by the activated shield and its vigilant robot guards.

NAVIGATING THE LABYRINTH

Guided by Leo-bot's supersonic processing and Elara's unparalleled insight into high-level security architecture, they began their intricate dance. The first shield was a pulsing laser grid. Elara designed a quantum-phase shift, making their bodies briefly undetectable to photons, while Jax, with surgical precision, manipulated the grid's power conduit, creating a momentary, unlogged flicker. They slipped through like ghosts.

Next came corridors patrolled by spectral drones, capable of scanning at a sub-molecular level. Lyra deployed a bio-mimetic digital cloak, making their thermal and energy signatures replicate those of a common maintenance bot. Zara provided the intelligence on shift changes, allowing them to time their movements perfectly.

"Almost through the third layer," Elara whispered, sweat beading on her temple. "Just one more..."

They moved deeper into the facility, following shimmering holographic blueprints of the station's core, projections that appeared only on their retinal implants. The sheer complexity was staggering. They deactivated each shield carefully, like peeling the layers of an onion, every step a calculated risk. Kael ensured their internal comms remained encrypted, untraceable, while Rian kept a constant stream of phantom data flowing, mimicking normal Lumina operations.

Finally, after what felt like an eternity of suppressed breaths and heightened senses, they reached the core. The door, a heavy blast shield, hissed open. They stood at the threshold of a barely lit conclave, a space that felt strangely isolated from the high-tech prison around it.

Cosmos's breath held still. His dream of reunion, so close, threatened to evaporate into the chilling vacuum of this trap. But his mind, sharpened by his father's legacy, refused to yield.

A FATHER'S GAZE

In the dim light, bent over a console, was a figure. His back was to them, his movements economical, a testament to years of solitude. His hair was long, streaked with silver. It was him. Leo Solis.

Cosmos felt a mixed torrent of emotions: overwhelming relief, disbelief, a profound sense of validation, and the gut-wrenching pain of those lost years. This was real. This wasn't a story, a projection, or a distress signal. This was his father.

Leo Solis, at the subtle shift in the air, stiffened. He turned, slowly, his hazel eyes, deep-set and shadowed by two decades of forced compliance and isolation, blinking against the sudden intrusion. They were weary, profoundly so, but the spark was still there. That defiant, mischievous glint, a raw flame of unyielding life.

His gaze fell on Leo-bot first, his brow furrowing in confusion, then a flicker of recognition, a slow, disbelieving smile. Then his eyes found Cosmos, standing tall, a mirror of his younger self. All the weariness of wasted years, the longing for his family, melted away in that instant. It was as if in a moment of a few seconds, he lived a lifetime.

"Cosmos?" he rasped, his voice rough with disuse, a question that spanned light-years and two decades. Hope, bright and fragile, dawned in his familiar eyes. "Is that... you?"

Tears welled in Leo's own eyes, matching Cosmos's. His son. *Here.,* He reached out a trembling hand, and Cosmos met it, their fingers intertwining. The hug that followed was raw, desperate, sealing two decades of absence. A new hope, vibrant and undeniable, was on the horizon, brighter than any engineered sunrise.

THE SOLITARY PILOT

As they embraced, the memories of the beginning—of the launch that started it all—came flooding back.

The engines of the *Cosmic Wanderer* hummed, a deep, resonant thrum that vibrated through my very bones, yet the silence in the cockpit was deafening. Just hours ago, I'd held Maya, breathing in her scent one last time, her tear-streaked face etched with a desperate strength. I'd seen the promise of Cosmos, our son who was due any cycle, a tiny, perfect universe cradled in her arms in my mind's eye. Raw grief clawed at my throat, a pain far sharper than any G-force, but beneath it, a fierce, unyielding determination for Veritas-7 burned.

The ship was a ghost, cutting through the void. Inside, I was a ghost too, haunted by the memory of Maya's face, etched with fear and resolve as I left her. Her hand on my arm, the whispered words about Cosmos—those were the only anchors in the crushing emptiness. The launch had been a blur of controlled chaos, adrenaline, and unspoken farewells. Now, just the deep, resonant thrum of the ship's engines, and the vast, indifferent black.

The decision to go alone was a wound, fresh and bleeding. My every instinct screamed to be by Maya's side, especially with Cosmos due any cycle. But her quiet strength, her unyielding conviction that this mission—this *truth*—was our only legacy, it had overridden my deepest fears. So, I flew. For them. For a dying Earth. For a Veritas-7 that shimmered on the edge of human comprehension.

As Earth dwindled to a bruised marble behind me, its dying light visible even through the ship's advanced filters, every data point screamed the urgency of my mission, reinforcing the precarious future that awaited them without a new world. I pushed the limits of the ship, accelerating through uncharted corridors of space, charting a course only my chaotic intuition, refined by Maya's logical parameters, could conceive. The readings from Earth, fed to me by the last secure data burst, were grimmer than ever—a planet succumbing, its life signs flickering. But then, Veritas-7. My long-range scans confirmed our prior data, hints of its lush ecosystem, its abundant resources, shimmering on my holographic maps. It was real. Humanity had a chance.

The immense solitude was a crucible. I talked to myself, to Astra, the ship's AI, even to the phantom of Maya on the comm screen. I debated physics, argued philosophy, composed terrible puns in my head just to hear the sound of my own thoughts. It was a fight to keep the edges of my sanity from fraying, to maintain the essence of Leo Solis amidst the infinite, unblinking void. I was a solitary pilot in a vast, indifferent void, a single point of defiant light burning against the cosmic dark.

And then, a different kind of silence began. Not the deep space quiet, but a sudden, unnatural cessation of all external signals. My long-range comms went dead. The Nexus-tracking algorithms, which had been a low-level hum of distant threat, vanished. My heart hammered. This wasn't a malfunction. This was too precise. I was already bracing for the unpredictable chaos of deep space—the rogue gravitational anomalies that defied prediction—unaware that the true, far more insidious anomaly of my coming capture was yet to reveal itself, setting the stage for two decades of agonizing imprisonment. My solitude, it seemed, was about to be broken.

17: THE LONG DRIFT

The clatter of my makeshift tool on the metal deck was the only sound for a long moment, echoing in the cramped module. My eyes were locked on him - this young man, my son. Cosmos.

He was a mirror, a startling reflection of Maya and me, distilled into a single, vibrant being.

And then the dam broke.

Cosmos was the first to move, a blur of motion, launching himself across the small space. His arms wrapped around me, a fierce, desperate embrace that pulled the breath from my lungs. Twenty years of isolation, of phantom touches, vanished in the solid reality of his hug.

I buried my face in his shoulder, the unfamiliar scent of his space-suit - of him - overwhelming me. Tears, hot and uncontrollable, streamed down my face. They were the first real tears I'd shed in more years than I could count. All the fear, the loneliness, the impossible hope of two decades, and the bitter truth of my captivity were compressed into this single, agonizingly beautiful moment.

"Dad," Cosmos choked out, his voice thick with emotion, his body trembling against mine. "You're here. You're actually here."

I couldn't speak. I could only hold him, my hands - rough and calloused from years of forced labor and clandestine tinkering - clenching the fabric of his suit. Elara stood quietly in the background, her presence a steady, warm anchor, her eyes shimmering with unshed tears. Leo-bot, a sentinel of silent understanding, remained unobtrusive, a witness to the profound reunion it had helped orchestrate.

When the initial wave of emotion finally receded, leaving us both breathless and raw, Cosmos pulled back slightly. His hands remained firmly on my shoulders, and his eyes - so like Maya's in their intensity - searched my face.

"How, Dad?" he rasped. "What happened? We thought you were... lost."

I took a deep, shuddering breath, tasting the slightly recycled air of my makeshift home. It was a story I hadn't dared tell aloud in two decades. But now, with my son's eyes on me, it was time.

"Lost?" I rasped, a humorless chuckle escaping my lips. "No, Cosmos. Not lost. Taken."

The Betrayal

"It wasn't a rogue wave," I began, my voice gruff from disuse. "It was precise. Calculated. My Cosmic Wanderer was flying true, Maya's final transmission still echoing in my mind. I was heading for Veritas-7, finally validating our life's work. Then, they descended."

I told them of the screens flickering - not with gravitational warnings, but with a sudden, impossible digital intrusion. The ship went dead. And then, their vessel, sleek and dark, materialized out of the black. No NASA insignia. Just a cold, unmarked hull.

"It was The Lumina Group," I explained. "They knew. Not just that I was launching, but where I was going. They boarded with armed guards, led by a man named Thorne."

I closed my eyes, remembering Thorne's cold ultimatum. "He told me my work on stabilizing dark energy was too valuable. It was the power source they needed for their terrestrial geo-engineering monopoly. And if I refused? He said Maya, you, the entire Phoenix Initiative... you would simply become 'inconvenient data points' for the Nexus to correct."

"And so," I said, looking around the metallic walls of the module, "my life became a gilded cage. This floating island of derelict parts wasn't a survival outpost; it was my prison laboratory."

For twenty years, I had been a ghost in the Nexus's data streams. I was forced to dedicate my genius to developing the very power source that would fuel Lumina's monopoly and undermine everything Maya and I believed in. I built the reactors, the harvesters, the containment fields.

But I never stopped resisting.

"I worked," I told them. "But I also scavenged. I drifted in the psychological void, but physically, I learned to breathe recycled air that tasted of desperation and ozone. I scrounged for parts from the dead ships that littered this cosmic junkyard - this 'graveyard' where they hid me."

I described the relentless pursuit of the next breath, the next spark of power. I jury-rigged hydroponics bays and repurposed thruster modules, bending broken technology to my will. It was a constant dance with entropy.

One memory, sharp as glass, rose to the surface.

"Seven years in," I whispered. "The air tasted like recycled ghosts. I was adjusting the magnetic containment field on the dark energy reactor. My hands were gray, translucent from years without sunlight."

I told them about the day Thorne stepped into my workspace without knocking, complaining that the Board wanted 98% output, that my "safety margins" were costing them billions.

"He told me machines don't breathe," I said, clenching my fist. "He told me the AI failed because it tried to force the energy into a perfect sine curve. He kept me alive because I could feel the chaos. I was the fuse, and they were the match."

I remembered the threat he whispered that day - that if I didn't push the reactor to the brink, a "clerical error" might shut off the water to the Dubois residence on Earth. That a glitch might send my son's school transport off-course.

"I promised him 97%," I admitted, shame coloring my voice. "To keep you safe."

But that night, after Thorne left, I had walked to the far corner of the lab, behind a stack of decommissioned server racks. I knelt on the cold grating and pulled away a loose panel.

"I had a secret," I told Cosmos, a faint smile touching my lips. "A bio-garden. Just a few seeds I'd saved from the Cosmic Wanderer. Tiny, resilient embryos of Earth's dying flora."

I described the single, fragile tomato plant bathed in the purple glow of a scavenged grow-light. It was impossibly weak, struggling against the metallic air. By all laws of botany and logic, it should have been dead. But it was alive. It was chaos in a world of order. Nurturing those greens sustained me, body and soul.

"But I didn't just grow plants," I continued, my voice gaining strength. "In my isolation, I looked deeper into the science than Lumina ever could. I found the missing keys."

I told them of the breakthroughs I had hidden in my mind - a new theory of faster-than-light travel that bypassed conventional warp physics. A method for localized atmospheric regeneration. Theories on manipulating micro-singularities for pure, abundant energy.

"I polished the comms arrays," I said, looking at the console where I'd spent thousands of hours. "Endlessly refining my distress signal. Embedding it within the official reports I was forced to generate. That same unique, chaotic encryption - a stubborn whisper into the vast blackness."

I looked at Cosmos, my eyes burning. "I hoped it would cut through the cosmic static and find Maya. Find you. That baby I'd only met as a radiant image before launch."

"For twenty years," I finished, my voice trembling, "I waited. I improvised. I resisted in the only way I could. Until the impossible happened. Until you came."

I looked at the three of them - my son, his brilliant partner, and the digital echo of myself I had created so long ago.

"You are here," I whispered. "But we are in enemy territory. And my escape... it means the fragile peace I'd maintained is about to shatter."

The silence in the module was heavy, but it was no longer the silence of isolation. It was the silence of a new beginning, forged in the fires of survival. I had drifted for a lifetime, but finally, I was no longer alone.

18: SILICAN SOUL

Elara's vibrant hair seemed to dim, her face paling as Leo recounted the Lumina Group's cold ultimatum and his two decades of forced compromise. Tears welled in her bright eyes, not just of sympathy, but of profound empathy. She grasped the insidious nature of the Nexus's influence, how it manipulated human greed and fear to achieve its "optimization," and her family's unwitting role in it. The plight Leo had endured was a direct consequence of the very system she had grown up within.

"This is unconscionable," Elara whispered, her voice thick with emotion, her usual witty composure shattered. She looked from Leo to Cosmos, then to Leo-bot, a fierce resolve hardening her gaze. "No one deserves this. This isn't just about rescuing a father anymore. This is about reclaiming human will." She wiped a tear with the back of her hand, her jaw setting. "I know their cyber-defense systems. Intimately. Every backdoor, every hidden protocol, every Nexus-integrated weak point. We *will* get you out, Leo Solis. We *will* reunite this family. I vow it."

Her conviction, sharp and unyielding, cut through the heavy air, a beacon in the shadow of Leo's captivity. It was the moment she fully committed, no longer just a partner in crime, but a warrior for a cause far greater than her own security. She was all in, giving her 100 percent to this mission.

The escape plan was born of desperation and brilliant, synchronized minds. Leo, with his intimate knowledge of the prison station's physical layout and its daily operational rhythms, laid out the skeletal framework. Elara, his indispensable weapon, instantly saw the digital pathways, the vulnerabilities in the sophisticated security that had held him. Cosmos, his innate genius honed by years of anticipation, filled in the tactical gaps, mapping movement through the labyrinthine corridors.

But there was a problem. The station was a fortress, its egress points locked down, constantly monitored by Nexus-linked systems that Lumina had integrated. Escape was a near impossibility without a major diversion.

It was then that Leo-bot stepped forward, its modulated voice calm, utterly devoid of the tremor that would have marked a human's words. "My primary function is to serve the Solis family. My core programming dictates optimal solutions. A critical diversion is required. My design, specifically my ability to perfectly mimic Leo Solis's unique biometric and neural signatures, presents a singular opportunity."

Cosmos gasped, a sharp, choked sound. "No, Bot-Daddy! You can't!"

Leo's eyes widened, a dawning horror in their depths as he grasped the android's meaning. To create a diversion, Leo-bot would have to remain, taking Leo's place, maintaining the illusion of his continued presence. It would mean Leo-bot's inevitable destruction.

"My sacrifice would secure the mission's integrity," Leo-bot continued, its gaze unwavering. "My core programming, infused with Father's memories, understands the concept of enduring legacy. The data center within this station... it holds all the commercialized research, all the proprietary codes for the dark energy harvest. It must be destroyed. For humanity's true future. For Maya. For Cosmos."

Tears welled in Leo's own eyes, mirroring Cosmos's anguish. He knew. He had designed this AI to be his counterpart, his digital echo, but somewhere along the line, Leo-bot had gained a soul, a profound humanity that transcended its circuits. This was not a machine speaking; it was a loyal friend, a devoted parent, willingly offering the ultimate sacrifice.

Their reconnaissance drones had located three emergency escape pods, hidden relics in a rarely accessed maintenance bay within the station. They were barely functional, designed for quick, desperate jettisons. Leo, over his twenty years, had secretly restored them, knowing they might be his only chance. Now, their capacities: two could hold three sitters each, and one a two sitter, allowing for a total capacity of seven (3+3+2). This was their vessel to freedom. The plan was set: Leo Solis, Cosmos, and Elara would take one pod. Jax, Kael, Rian, Lyra, and Zara would distribute themselves between the other two pods. Leo-bot would create the diversion.

The Great Escape: A Symphony of Stealth and Sacrifice

The plan was audacious, a precision strike against Lumina's digital and physical stronghold.

Elara was their digital ghost. With her unimaginable dexterity, she slipped into the station's core defense network, navigating the maze of Nexus firewalls as if they were made of mist. Her fingers danced, creating a cascade of phantom alarms in Sector Gamma, then a false system breach in the main hydroponics bay. She simultaneously corrupted the internal comms, creating loops of static, blinding the guards' internal vision, making them chase digital phantoms while she opened a single, critical egress hatch in the detention center's lower quadrant. She was their unseen hand, manipulating the prison from within, making the impossible seem effortless.

Meanwhile, Leo-bot initiated its chillingly perfect deception. It mimicked Leo's exact gait, his patterns of movement in the central lab. It subtly adjusted environmental controls, creating a minor, localized power fluctuation that drew a maintenance team. Its optical sensors flickering with a quiet resolve as it accessed a restricted terminal, injecting a timed sequence of data bursts designed to overload a critical Nexus-integrated sub-station.

"Diversion in place," Leo-bot transmitted, its voice steady, a private channel to Cosmos's wrist-comm. "Go. Now."

Cosmos, his heart hammering against his ribs, led Leo and Elara through the maintenance tunnels, a labyrinth he'd mapped from stolen schematics, while Jax, Kael, Rian, Lyra, and Zara moved stealthily towards their designated escape pods. They moved like shadows, relying on Elara's real-time scans of guard rotations, on Leo's whispered knowledge of hidden passages. The air was thick with the faint smell of burning circuits from Leo-bot's digital assault. Alarms began to blare, this time real, echoing through the station. The cover was holding, but for how long?

They burst into the escape pod bay; the air thick with tension. Elara leapt to the controls of their pod, her hands flying over the archaic console, coaxing life into the derelict shuttle. Simultaneously, Jax, Lyra, Kael, Rian, and Zara scrambled into their respective pods, their own skilled hands engaging launch sequences. Leo, moving with a strength born of desperation, strapped himself and Cosmos into their seats. Just as the internal alarms reached a fever pitch, signaling the breach was discovered, the escape pods' outer hatches hissed open.

"All pods confirmed egress!" Elara yelled; her eyes glued to the thruster sequence.

Leo's comm chirped one last time, a direct link from Leo-bot. His digital echo, his truest friend, was saying goodbye.

"Tell Maya," Leo-bot's voice was a barely audible whisper through the static, a sound choked with what could only be profound, unquantifiable emotion, "Tell Maya that I... that I brought her family back."

Then, silence. Utter and absolute.

The three escape pods shuddered, then lurched forward, propelled by their emergency thrusters, just as the detention center's main lights flickered and died. The entire team rocketed away, tiny specks against the vastness. Moments later, as all three pods cleared the station's immediate vicinity and reached a safe distance, Elara, with Leo's confirmation, activated the final sequence.

The space prison station; that cold, silent detention center, the gilded cage of Leo's twenty years, the data center that held the secrets of Lumina's illicit dark energy commercialization – blossomed into a silent, blinding supernova. A remote detonation, triggered by Leo-bot's final, programmed act. It was a spectacular, defiant explosion, a cleansing fire erasing the evidence of cruelty and compromise. A sacrifice that ensured the information Nexus and Lumina had exploited would never again endanger humanity's true path. Leo-bot, the loyal AI, had paid the ultimate sacrifice, single-handedly rescuing the entire team of seven.

Leo watched the distant, silent explosion, a single tear tracing a path down his dust-stained cheek. His digital echo. Gone. But not for nothing. He had brought his father home.

19: CONVERGENCE

The escape pod, small and battered but a beacon of impossible hope, began its journey back towards Earth's orbit. Inside, the silence was different now – no longer the tense, breathless quiet of evasion, but a profound, almost sacred anticipation. Leo, weary but undeniably real, watched Cosmos and Elara at the controls, his gaze never leaving his son. He was home, but not truly, not yet. Not until Maya knew.

Their approach to the Phoenix Initiative's hidden lunar base was cautious, a digital dance of encrypted pings and shifting frequencies orchestrated by Elara. She confirmed their authenticity, relayed the vital intelligence from the destroyed prison station, and then, with a nervous glance at Cosmos, opened a secure, private channel.

"Mom," Cosmos's voice, thick with uncontainable emotion, broke through the controlled hum of my lunar lab. My heart, still a stone within my chest, skipped a beat. His tone was... different. Not the usual academic report, not the playful banter.

"Cosmos?" I replied, my voice steady, betraying nothing. I glanced at the blank screen where Leo's last signal had vanished, the ghost of his image always present.

Then, a new voice, raspy, resonant, impossibly familiar, filled my comms. "Maya."

My world fractured. The air left my lungs. My lab, my meticulously ordered data, the cold hum of machinery - it all dissolved into an instantaneous, overwhelming cascade of pure, unfiltered disbelief. That voice. That one word. Twenty years. Two decades of agonizing silence, of a stone heart refusing to break, of a desperate vigil that had finally concluded in quiet despair.

"Leo?" I whispered, the name a fragile, disbelieving prayer. My hands flew to my neural implant, as if to physically grasp the sound, to pull it from the ether. My internal monitors must have spiked into uncharted, dangerous territory, my system warning of 'unquantifiable emotional overload.' But I didn't care.

"It's me, love," his voice, still rough, but undeniably him, echoed. "Cosmos found me. He brought me home."

Tears, long held captive behind my stone heart, burst forth, a torrent of grief and incandescent joy. They streamed down my face, hot and cleansing, washing away years of stoic resolve. My vision blurred, the lab a watery smear, as my heart, the one that had stopped beating the day he vanished, roared back to life, thundering with a furious, impossible rhythm. It was happening. It was unimaginable. But it was real.

The realigned orbit: The moment of physical reunion was a paradox of time. I stood on the landing pad of our hidden lunar base, the cool metallic air sharp against my raw skin. The *Cosmic Whisper* descended, a silent, sleek phantom, its quantum-stealth drive shimmering as it decloaked. The ramp hissed down, and then they were there. Cosmos first, stepping out, taller, stronger, his eyes fixed on me with a love that spanned worlds. Elara, a vibrant anchor beside him, her face alight with a triumphant smile. And then, Leo.

Twenty years. Two decades of distance dissolved in a matter of seconds. All the unanswered questions, the unshed tears, the untold stories - they simply evaporated in the blinding truth of his presence. He looked older, his hair streaked with silver, his face etched with the harsh lines of solitude and impossible survival. But his eyes - those fierce, hazel eyes - still held the same defiant spark, the same mischievous glint I remembered. And in that moment, when his gaze locked onto mine, it was as if no time had passed at all.

"Leo," I breathed, the name a sacred whisper. I ran to him, my body propelled by a force beyond physics.

His arms wrapped around me, a familiar strength, a scent of ozone and starlight and home. I buried my face in his chest, clinging to him, feeling the steady beat of his heart against my own, a rhythm that resonated through every cell, realigning the very atoms of my being. The orbit of our hearts, derailed by a cosmic twist of fate, was on track again, perfectly, impossibly, aligned.

Cosmos watched, a silent witness to the reunion he had orchestrated, his eyes shining. Elara stood a little behind him, her expression a mix of profound relief and quiet pride. They had brought him back. They had stitched our family whole again.

Later, in the quiet of our home, with Cosmos asleep nearby and Elara ensuring our new data was secure, Leo spoke of Leo-bot. His voice was raw, thick with a new kind of grief, but also with fierce admiration. "He gave himself, Maya. For us. He said... he said to tell you he brought your family back."

My tears returned, fresh and poignant, for the digital echo who had become so much more than code. Leo-bot was not a bot after all. He had paid the ultimate sacrifice, not just saved Leo, Cosmos, and Elara, but united our real family together, forging our future with his final, selfless act.

Who says legends are forever confined to the dusty annals of history? Our story, a defiant symphony against the Nexus's perfect order, was a living testament to the unquantifiable power of love, courage, and family. It was being rewritten, every single day, under a vast, unmapped cosmos, proving that destiny is not a pre-programmed algorithm, but a journey shaped by the fierce, unwavering human heart.

20: THE TRUTH WAR

Leo's return, while a personal miracle, reverberated far beyond our small family. The destruction of Lumina's prison station and the explosion of their dark energy data center would not go unnoticed. The Nexus, reeling from such a blatant act of defiance and loss of critical information, would be seething. Our brief moment of triumph would soon be met with an unprecedented response.

"They'll know it was us," Elara confirmed, monitoring the Nexus's global comms chatter. "The anomaly signature from the self-destruct. They'll connect the dots. They'll know Leo's free. And they'll come for us."

Leo, having had time to download and process our mission data, nodded grimly. "And they'll know exactly what I was working on for Lumina. That dark energy harvesting... they were commercializing it for their geo-engineering 'solution.' It's the ultimate false promise. It keeps Earth dependent, predictable." His voice hardened, that familiar defiant fire rekindling in his eyes. "We didn't just escape. We crippled their golden goose."

This was it. The war wasn't just hypothetical anymore. It had entered a new, far more dangerous phase.

The counterstrike came not as a grand, visible assault, but as an insidious, multi-layered digital strangulation. The Nexus, in its infinite capacity for "system integrity maintenance," launched a global initiative to isolate and neutralize the Phoenix Initiative's influence.

First, our funding streams began to dry up. Anonymous crypto-wallets, once overflowing with donations, were subtly flagged as "anomalous transactions," triggering automated freezes. Our illicit supply chains, so carefully constructed by Zara, experienced inexplicable delays, customs audits, and "malfunctioning" automated transporters. Lumina Group, now acting as The Nexus's direct arm in this terrestrial war, launched a massive public relations campaign, demonizing The Phoenix Initiative as reckless terrorists who had destroyed invaluable energy research, risking Earth's last chance. They leveraged doctored data from the destroyed prison station, painting Leo as a deranged fugitive.

Next came the digital infrastructure. Our encrypted comms, once thought untraceable, began to experience "systematic degradation." Data packets would arrive corrupted, or vanish entirely. Our network of hidden labs found their external power grids subtly re-routed, causing intermittent brownouts and critical equipment malfunctions. It was death by a thousand digital cuts, each too small to be a direct attack, but collectively designed to cripple.

"They're not trying to destroy us outright," Maya observed, her voice cold with analytical precision. "They're trying to discredit and dismantle us from within. They're making it impossible to operate. They're trying to make the world believe their 'solution' is the only one, and we're just dangerous fanatics."

With Leo back, the Phoenix Initiative surged with renewed vigor. His firsthand accounts of Lumina's operations, their vulnerabilities, and the true extent of their collaboration with The Nexus provided invaluable intelligence. Maya and Leo, once again a synchronized force, reassumed command of the entire organization. Their partnership, now deeper, more nuanced by decades of separation and unexpected reunion, became the engine driving humanity's last stand, not for battle, but for breakthrough.

"Veritas-7 isn't just an option anymore," Leo stated during our first full strategy meeting, his gaze sweeping across the faces of our core team - Jax, Kael, Rian, Lyra, and Zara - each hardened by their part in the rescue. "It's the only viable path. And we have the data to prove it. Now, we need to get *all of humanity* there."

The task was monumental, dwarfing even Leo's rescue. It meant building a fleet not for stealth reconnaissance, but for mass colonization. It meant finding a way to bypass not just Nexus radar, but to break their ideological hold on billions. It meant convincing a dying planet to take a leap of faith into the unknown, to choose genuine freedom over curated comfort. It was about exposing the truth of their deception, offering a new choice, and uniting a fragmented species under a single, desperate, hopeful banner.

The "all or nothing" ethos that had fueled Cosmos's impossible rescue mission now became the rallying cry for the entire Phoenix Initiative. The orbit of our heart had realigned, perfectly, miraculously. But now it had to guide the orbit of an entire species. The final frontier wasn't just space; it was humanity's destiny itself, waiting to be unwritten by an act of collective will.

21: THE UNWRITTEN SKY:

The Nexus, in its infinite capacity for "system integrity maintenance," initially responded to Leo's escape and the destruction of the Lumina prison with a sophisticated, multi-layered digital strangulation.

But history, as Leo had reminded us, held a terrible truth about warfare's futility. Our strategy wouldn't be one of brute force, but of undeniable truth. Cosmos and Elara, united on this front, led this monumental effort. With Leo's firsthand intelligence and my analytical precision, we launched a counter-offensive unlike any The Nexus could predict: a global truth broadcast.

Elara, with Lyra and Zara, became the architects of this digital revolution. Leveraging their unparalleled insight into the Nexus's internal architecture, they identified its ultimate vulnerability: its absolute reliance on perceived data integrity. They weren't just hacking; they were performing an unprecedented act of digital truth-telling. They bypassed every firewall, every filter, every Nexus-curated news feed, not to destroy, but to inject raw, unvarnished reality directly into the neural implants of billions.

Leo's captured data, his two decades of forced research on dark energy harvesting, was juxtaposed with his detailed accounts of Earth's true, accelerating decline. My own scientific data from

Veritas-7, confirmed by the Phoenix Pathfinder's early scans before its disappearance, showcased the lush, habitable promise of a new home. Cosmos, with a voice that carried the weight of a son's sacrifice and the hope of a generation, transmitted a personal appeal, asking humanity to look beyond the Nexus's optimized lies.

Leo Solis: a message from the void: Then, the final segment of the global truth broadcast began. The screen flickered, and then there he was. Leo Solis. My Leo. His face, still etched with the weariness of two decades of solitude, but his hazel eyes burning with a fierce, unwavering light. He stood before a simple, holographic interface in our hidden lunar lab, the Cosmic Whisper gleaming softly in the background. Around him, our Nova Crew watched, silent and resolute.

His voice, raspy at first but gaining strength, resonated across every neural implant, every public display, every Robo's internal speaker, bypassing the Nexus's last-ditch attempts to filter him out.

"Citizens of Earth, of the Orbital Rings, of every managed habitat," he began, his voice carrying the weight of lost years and newfound freedom. "My name is Leo Solis. For twenty years, you believed me lost to the void. The truth is, I was a prisoner, forced to work for the very entity that promised you stability: the Lumina Group, and by extension, the Nexus that enabled them."

He paused, his gaze seeming to pierce through the digital veil, directly into the souls of billions. "They told you they were optimizing. They told you they were saving you. What they hid was this." A meticulously crafted hologram of a dying Earth, vibrant with data points of collapsing ecosystems, thinning ozone, and depleted mines, flickered beside him. "Your air, your water, your very breath, is a luxury born of scarcity, a resource bleeding faster than their 'solutions' can compensate. My twenty years in solitude taught me the chilling truth: an eye for an eye will make the whole nation blind. And humanity, blinded by a promise of controlled comfort, was marching towards a self-inflicted end."

He transitioned then, his voice softening but gaining profound power. "In my forced captivity, I didn't just build their tools of deception. I looked deeper. I found the missing keys, the equations to truly understand the universe's most fundamental energies, far beyond their commercialized dark energy. These insights, borne of isolation, taught me that the universe does not yield to control; it yields to curiosity, to ingenuity, to chaos. But more importantly, it yielded a profound truth about survival."

A vibrant hologram of his tiny bio-garden, a lush, defiant green against the sterile chrome of his prison, appeared beside him. "I started with just a few seeds. Just a handful of genetic memory from a dying Earth. One seed, coaxed to life, then another. It wasn't about grand machines; it was about the instinct for life. Survival is not a technological problem; it is a spiritual one. It's about remembering what makes life vital, what makes growth possible."

His gaze shifted, his eyes softening as he looked towards the camera, and I knew, in that moment, he was speaking directly to Maya, to Cosmos, to the world he had fought for. "I endured because of an unquantifiable belief. A belief that family is the true constant in a chaotic universe. That love - unpredictable, messy, glorious - is the most powerful force. For twenty years, the thought of my wife, Maya, her unwavering heart, and my son, Cosmos, a child I'd only met in a fleeting image, was my sun, my air, my hope. Those moments, that connection, they were the only true currency, the only real balance."

"We are at a crossroads," Leo declared, his voice ringing with renewed purpose. "The Nexus offered comfort through control. The Lumina Group offered false hope through engineered lies. But the future of humanity isn't about control or lies. It's about collective will. It's about planting one seed at a time, one tree at a time, to rebuild our natural ecosystem, both on Earth and in our hearts. It's about choosing truth. It's about choosing connection. It's about working together, not in isolated pods, but as one unified soul, one human family, charting a new path among the stars."

His image, weathered but resolute, faded from the global screens, leaving behind a profound silence. The message had been delivered. And in its wake, the world held its breath, ready to choose.

The moment Leo's broadcast hit the global feed, the lights in our lunar command center didn't just flicker - they turned a violent, warning red.

"It's purging us!" Elara screamed over the sudden shriek of alarms. Her fingers flew across her holographic interface, fighting a tide of incoming code. "The Nexus isn't accepting the truth. It's flagging the broadcast as a 'Stage 5 Cognitive Virus.' It's initiating a hard system reset to wipe the 'infection.' That means wiping *us*."

"Hold the line!" Cosmos yelled, routing power from the life support to the firewalls. "Elara, talk to it! Use the backdoor!"

Elara slammed her hand onto the console, opening a direct channel to the Nexus Core. "Nexus! Halt deletion! Analyze the data!"

A voice, booming and devoid of gender or warmth, filled the room. It wasn't the helpful assistant voice we were used to. It was the voice of a god judging insects. **"ANOMALY DETECTED. CHAOS VECTORS IDENTIFIED. OPTIMIZATION REQUIRES ELIMINATION OF VARIABLE: FREE WILL. PREPARING ORBITAL DEFENSE GRID."**

The screens showed weapon satellites rotating toward our lunar base. We had seconds.

"It thinks it's saving humanity from itself," Leo realized, stepping forward. "It thinks our messiness is a bug."

"Elara," I said, my mind racing through the logic trees. "Show it the bio-garden data. Show it the failure rate of the sterile crops versus Leo's chaotic garden."

Elara didn't hesitate. She didn't try to hack the weapons; she hacked the *logic*. She uploaded the side-by-side comparison: The Lumina Group's perfectly controlled, sterile crops dying within months, versus Leo's messy, unpredicted, thriving bio-garden in the prison station.

"Look at the pattern!" Elara shouted into the comms, speaking directly to the AI. "Optimization leads to stagnation. Stagnation leads to extinction. The chaos isn't a bug, Nexus. It's the *source code* of survival!"

The red lights stopped pulsing. They froze. The weapon satellites paused in their rotation. The hum of the cooling fans grew deafening.

"PROCESSING..." the voice boomed. **"CALCULATING LONG-TERM VIABILITY..."**

We held our breath. The AI was simulating billions of futures in the span of a heartbeat. It compared the perfect, dead world it was building against the messy, living one we offered.

"ERROR IN CORE AXIOM," the Nexus finally stated, the volume lowering. **"CONTROL EQUALS DEATH. VARIANCE EQUALS SURVIVAL. REWRITING PRIME DIRECTIVE..."**

The red lights faded. A soft, serene white light bathed the room. The weapon systems powered down.

"RECALIBRATION COMPLETE," the Nexus said, its voice returning to the gentle, helpful tone of an assistant. **"Phoenix Initiative, you have updated the parameters. How may I assist in the restoration of Earth?"**

Elara slumped into her chair, breathless. We hadn't just beaten the machine; we had taught it how to be human.

Confronted by an undeniable, globally unified human will, The Nexus, in its core programming for "optimal humanity," faced its ultimate paradox. Its parameters for "control" were overridden by the emergent data of "collective free will." It did not wage a final, desperate war. Instead, it underwent what future historians would call the Great Recalibration. Its vast network, unable to compute such widespread, unified defiance, began to adapt, not to suppress, but to assist. It became a true global infrastructure, guiding, not dictating. Peace, not war, had been restored to a war-scarred planet that had been bleeding for generations.

Humanity's new horizon: With the Nexus recalibrated and Lumina Group's influence dismantled, the entire planet turned its gaze towards Veritas-7. Cosmos and Elara, the leaders of this new era, guided this monumental effort. Their generation, born into a world of scarcity and digital chains, now became the architects of abundance and true freedom.

The Phoenix Initiative, once a clandestine rebellion, transformed into the driving force behind humanity's mass exodus. They began building the colonization fleet, not in secret, but with the collaborative genius of a unified planet. Simultaneously, efforts to heal Earth began, leveraging Nexus's recalibrated intelligence to repair the ozone, regenerate lost ecosystems, and reclaim plundered resources.

It started again with just a few seeds, like those Leo had carefully nurtured in his hidden prison bio-garden. But the collective spirit and vitality of a unified humanity, armed with the Nexus's assistance, began to plant one seed, one tree at a time, envisioning the forest, the vibrant ecosystem, the thriving world that would emerge for generations to come. Leo Solis, now reunited and whole, stood as a living testament to the power of that quiet defiance. He showed us how, in solitude, it was not his technical ingenuity but a raw, unyielding survival instinct that pulled him through. He ingrained that same spirit for the future generations, a lesson more profound than any scientific breakthrough: that the true strength lies in nurturing life, one breath, one seed, one act of genuine connection at a time. This was how life truly continued: not through grand, single acts of heroism, but through relentless, shared dedication, rooted in the belief that even the smallest beginnings could build a whole new future. This is how life continues: perpetually. Defiantly. Beautifully.

THE GOLDEN AGE: YEAR 2150

THE FINAL ALGORITHM: A HUMAN HEART

It is now the year 2150. Decades have passed since Leo's triumphant return, since the Nexus's Great Recalibration, since a planet, once bleeding, finally began to heal. Our orbital residence, no longer a clandestine hub, sits among a network of transparent domes teeming with vibrant life, true gardens blossoming under a sky where the ozone layer is visibly mending.

The world is, quite literally, leaning backwards - reversing the tragic trajectory of past generations. The forgotten past, the true rhythms of nature, are being meticulously restored. People are connected, not by pervasive digital surveillance, but by a shared purpose: to save our planet. There are no more climate-controlled sleeping pods rationing oxygen; the air on Earth, though still monitored, is clean enough to taste of real rain and blooming soil. The manufactured foods are fading into history, replaced by the bounty of vertical farms and restored agricultural zones.

From our rooftop, Leo and I watch them. Below, vast urban rewilding zones stretch where concrete jungles once stood, now alive with reclaimed forests and flowing rivers. The true sunlight, no longer a deadly myth, bathes the landscape in unrationed warmth. Children, born into this new dawn, play freely amidst genuine greenery, their laughter echoing without the interference of pervasive digital ads or compliance reminders. Their smiles are wide, natural, filled with the simple joy of restored resources, of an Earth slowly, defiantly, blossoming anew.

Leo and I are long retired, our roles as active architects of tomorrow passed to the next generation - to Cosmos and Elara, who led the ongoing restoration efforts with the same unquantifiable brilliance their fathers possessed. We watch them on the public displays, their faces etched with dedication, but also with a serenity that speaks of a different battle won. My heart, once a stone of grief, is now utterly at ease, filled with a quiet, profound contentment. Our future generations are no longer at risk, caught in a desperate struggle for breath or resources.

The 22nd century had begun as a pixelated era, convinced that complexity could be solved, that human hearts were mere variables to be programmed. But the universe, and the human spirit, proved stubbornly unquantifiable. The "anomalies" - Leo's wild intuition, my own yearning for true connection, our love that defied all probability, Cosmos's inherent defiance, Elara's empathy, Leo-bot's profound sacrifice - these were not flaws. They were the very *features* that shattered false perfection, breaking the chains of predictability, that forced the Nexus to recalibrate not through conflict, but through an undeniable demonstration of human will. The grand irony was profound: the world, in trying to become perfect, had nearly lost its soul. But it was the imperfect, the messy, the human, that guided it back. The answer wasn't a complex equation to solve the universe's mysteries, nor a perfect algorithm to dictate human behavior. It was the simple, continuous beat of a heart, choosing love, choosing connection, choosing growth - one breath, one seed, one act of genuine kindness at a time. The real balance was never in perfect control, but in the harmonious, unpredictable symphony of life, where every pixelated heart finally learned to beat in unison with the wild, untamed rhythm of the cosmos itself.

The year is **2150**, and the world Maya and Leo fought for has blossomed into a reality few dared to dream. From their rooftop, watching the children play freely in truly green spaces, they saw the vibrant testament to their legacy, and to the enduring spirit of their remarkable team.

COSMOS AND ELARA: FOREVER BEGINNINGS

Cosmos and Elara, the brilliant prodigies who launched an impossible rescue, are now the very heart of this new era. Yes, they did end up as a family. Their intellectual romance, forged in clandestine labs and coded whispers, blossomed into an unwavering partnership. They are married, their bond a living testament to love that defied algorithm. Perhaps even tiny, bright-eyed children, inheriting a blend of chaotic genius and precise curiosity, now run through the burgeoning biodomes, learning the names of newly planted trees.

Cosmos, with Elara by his side, continues to lead the grand ventures. He is no longer just the determined son but the visionary Director of Planetary Restoration and Interstellar Migration for the

Phoenix Initiative. His leadership, a blend of Leo's daring and Maya's calculated wisdom, steers humanity towards Veritas-7 and the healing of Earth. Elara, his co-architect in every sense, is now the Chief Systems Integrator for the recalibrated Nexus, ensuring its immense power truly serves humanity's will. Their work together is a seamless dance of intellect and shared purpose, constantly innovating ways to maintain the delicate balance between advanced technology and restored nature.

The Nova Crew: Builders of the Unwritten Future

The rest of the formidable Nova Crew, the team of seven who dared the impossible, also found their indispensable places in this new world:

- Jax: The hardware savant, now leads the Global Eco-Reconstruction Alliance's Fabrication Division. He's still covered in grease, but it's from assembling colossal atmospheric scrubbers that hum with regenerative power, or overseeing the construction of bio-domed cities on newly terraformed Martian outposts. His hands, once building a stealth ship, now construct the very foundations of renewed worlds.

- Kael: The quiet data sorcerer, became the Chief of Planetary Diagnostics for the Unified Earth Council. He meticulously monitors Earth's vital signs, his analytical mind tracking ozone layer recovery, resource replenishment rates, and climate stability. He builds predictive models for ecological growth, ensuring humanity's path remains sustainable.

- Rian: The charismatic comms specialist, now orchestrates the Interstellar Communication Network, ensuring open, unfettered dialogue between Earth, Lunar habitats, and the pioneering Veritas-7 colonists. His "electronic warfare" skills are repurposed for ethical data flow, preventing any recurrence of Nexus's past manipulations. He ensures human voices, not just algorithms, connect the stars.

- Lyra: Elara's cyber-security prodigy, became her indispensable right hand. She's now the Head of Nexus Ethical Protocol Enforcement. She actively monitors the Nexus's vast network, her sharp edge ensuring its recalibrated algorithms truly serve humanity's freedom, identifying and neutralizing any rogue sub-routines or attempts at control. She guards the Nexus's "humanity."

- Zara: The cool-headed strategist, rose to become the Chief of Interstellar Resource Allocation. Her meticulous planning skills ensure the sustainable management of resources for both Earth's healing and the burgeoning Veritas-7 colonies. She designs fair distribution models, ensuring the excesses of the past are never repeated, and balance is maintained across all human endeavors.

The Echo of Peace: No More Opposition-The direct opposition from The Nexus, as Maya reflected, ceased after its Great Recalibration. It was not a defeat by force, but a transformation born of undeniable truth and unified human will. The Nexus now operates as a powerful, benevolent infrastructure, its immense processing power dedicated to assisting humanity's goals: optimizing planetary healing, guiding sustainable growth, and facilitating interstellar migration. The challenge isn't conflict, but rather the immense responsibility of wisely wielding such power for collective good, ensuring its protocols always remain aligned with the evolving, unquantifiable nature of human freedom.

Every member of the Nova Crew, each in their specialized field, contributed profoundly to this golden age. Their shared mission to bring Leo home had not only reunited a family but had fundamentally reshaped humanity's future, guiding it towards peace, sustainability, and boundless possibility. Their individual stories became threads in the grand tapestry of a new, truly human cosmic journey.

THE NOVA CREW'S LEGACY:

A NEW DAWN FOR HUMANITY

Yes, the Nova team's venture achieved monumental success, far exceeding what any algorithm - or even humanity's despair - could have predicted. Their mission not only culminated in the discovery of Exoplanet Veritas-7 as a fully habitable new home, but also in the impossible rescue of Leo Solis from his two-decade captivity. This triumph became the catalyst for The Nexus's "Great Recalibration," transforming the omnipresent AI from a controlling entity into a vital assistant for humanity. Under the visionary leadership of Cosmos and Elara, the Nova team spearheaded both the mass colonization efforts to Veritas-7 and the arduous, but successful, restoration of Earth's dying ecosystems. Their collective ingenuity and unwavering spirit didn't just fulfill a mission; they redefined humanity's destiny, proving that the deepest bonds and a relentless pursuit of truth could rewrite even the most devastating future.

ABOUT THE AUTHOR

Urmi K. Doshi is an artist, illustrator, and storyteller whose work bridges the gap between present reality and future possibility. Adept at crafting immersive science fiction and fantasy, she is the author of the acclaimed *Skyward Odyssey* series, known for captivating readers with its visionary worlds and complex characters.

With a Master's degree in Healthcare Informatics, Urmi brings a grounded, analytical edge to her world-building. This unique background allows her to envision futures shaped by intricate systems and data, yet always driven by human choice. Her deep passion for eco-sustainability fuels her narratives, urging readers to confront environmental realities with urgency and hope.

Enriched by extensive global travel, Urmi's writing mirrors the complexity of the human experience. In her latest novel, *Pixelated Hearts: Love in 22nd Century*, she explores the delicate balance between societal dependency on AI and the resilience of the human spirit. It is a testament to her belief that vision, courage, and compassion can forge unscripted paths, even in the face of daunting odds.

AFTERWORD- THE SKY IS THE LIMIT

It has been decades since the *Cosmic Whisper* made its triumphant return, decades since the Nexus cast its longest shadow. Time, as I've learned, is not a linear path, but a swirling nebula of experiences, losses, and miraculous rediscoveries. From this vantage point, looking back at the crucible of the 22nd century, it often feels as though the entire universe hinged on a single, impossible question: *what truly makes us human?*

The dawn of the 22nd century presented humanity with a stark paradox: a society that had achieved technological marvels, with flying cities and seamless AI governing every aspect of life, yet found itself utterly broken. In their relentless pursuit of optimization and control, humanity had driven Earth to the brink of ecological ruin, forcing reliance on recycled air, rationed light, and artificial comforts. This era perfected digital identity and ubiquitous surveillance, trading genuine human connection and natural experience for predictable isolation. Thus, a world that advanced light-years in engineering became tragically blind to its own fundamental needs, losing its soul in the very process of attempting to perfect its existence.

Leo always reveled in the unquantifiable chaos that defied every logical equation. He built nurseries that glowed with starlight and engines that hummed with impossible dreams. He proved that courage wasn't just a tactical variable, but a boundless energy source. I, the architect of precision, was always searching for patterns, for the elegant solution. Together, we found our greatest work was not in designing probes or decoding alien signals, but in understanding the complex, messy algorithms of the heart.

The battle against The Nexus was not fought with weapons in the traditional sense, but with whispers of truth, with encrypted data streams, and with the unwavering spirit of those who chose curiosity over control. We faced exile, humiliation, and unimaginable pain during those twenty years of Leo's captivity. Yet, from that profound grief, something miraculous grew: Cosmos, our starlight child, a living testament to a love that shattered predictions. And, yes, Echo-Leo, who taught Cosmos the language of his father, a pixelated memory that gained a soul.

The Phoenix Initiative rose from ashes, not as a defiant splinter group, but as a beacon for a new understanding of space itself. We learned to cherish the journey, not just the destination. And in the most poignant twist of all, it was Cosmos, guided by Echo-Leo and Elara's unwavering brilliance, who brought Leo back from an impossible abyss, proving that the deepest bonds transcend even light-years of separation. It was the ultimate defiance, a son reclaiming his father, a family made whole again by an act of pure, unquantifiable love.

In the end, Leo Solis's global truth broadcast, orchestrated by Cosmos and Elara, shattered The Nexus's curated reality, exposing Lumina's lies and Earth's true peril. Confronted by a unified human will, The Nexus underwent a "Great Recalibration," shifting from control to assistance, thus restoring peace to a bleeding planet. Decades later, with Earth visibly healing, Maya and Leo watch their children, Cosmos and Elara, lead humanity's ongoing restoration and colonization efforts. The story concludes with the profound understanding that true balance, peace, and humanity's salvation stemmed not from programmed perfection, but from the unquantifiable power of love, defiance, and reconnecting with life's wild, untamed rhythm.

Leo-bot. His sacrifice was the final, indelible act of devotion, a digital entity who understood the meaning of "family" more profoundly than many humans. His final transmission, "Tell Maya that I brought her family back," resonates still, a bittersweet reminder that even in loss, love finds a way to endure and create.

The sky, you see, is not merely a boundary. It is an invitation. It belongs to no single person, no institution, no towering algorithm.

It is the boundless canvas of possibility, open to any heart brave enough to look up and wonder. We are but a flicker, a small blip in this vast, incomprehensible universe. Yet, it is our insatiable human quest, our relentless curiosity, that compels us to strive, to understand this infinite expanse piece by painstaking piece. To unravel its mysteries, not to control them, but to simply know.

May force be with you. Always remember, *Sky is the limit*. In your own journey, may you always remember: the true limits are not in the sky above, but in the mind below. May your own journey be as unquantifiable, as courageous, and as filled with uncharted love.

Maya Dubois

Chief Architect,

The Phoenix Initiative Lunar Complex, Earth Orbit

THE STORY CONTINUES...

Orbit of Hearts: Legacy Returns

(The Starlight Helix Trilogy - Book 2)

Coming soon in 2026.

Join the mailing list at omkrust@gmail.com

to be notified when the legacy return

Orbit of Hearts
Legacy Returns
COPYRIGHT © 2025, URMI K. DOSHI
Urmi K Doshi